MALL MASSACRE

Holden saw one of the terrorists duck for cover into the front of a card-and-gift shop. He walked toward it, glass crunching under his feet, the M16 in his right fist.

And then he saw the man, a young woman in front of him like a shield.

"Don't mess with me, man!"

"Let her go!" Holden brought the rifle to his shoulder, his left arm screaming pain as he moved it. The distance was less than ten yards. Holden moved the selector to semi, his finger touching the trigger as the girl—a blonde, in her early twenties—screamed. Holden fired.

The FLNAer's head seemed to explode, a wash of blood belching up and back from it, becoming a sick pinkish cloud of spray as the girl fell to her knees screaming and the FLNAer collapsed into a heap.

Holden lowered the rifle, his shoulders slumping. He began to walk, slowly, back toward the fountain.

The water was running red.

QUANTITY SALES

Most Dell books are available at special quantity discounts when purchased in bulk by corporations, organizations, and special-interest groups. Custom imprinting or excerpting can also be done to fit special needs. For details write: Dell Publishing, 666 Fifth Avenue, New York, NY 10103. Attn.: Special Sales Department.

INDIVIDUAL SALES

Are there any Dell books you want but cannot find in your local stores? If so, you can order them directly from us. You can get any Dell book in print. Simply include the book's title, author, and ISBN number if you have it, along with a check or money order (no cash can be accepted) for the full retail price plus $1.50 to cover shipping and handling. Mail to: Dell Readers Service, P.O. Box 5057, Des Plaines, IL 60017.

THE

BATTLE
BEGINS

Jerry Ahern

A DELL BOOK

Published by
Dell Publishing
a division of
The Bantam Doubleday Dell Publishing Group, Inc.
1 Dag Hammarskjold Plaza
New York, New York 10017

The trademark Dell® is registered in the
U. S. Patent and Trademark Office.

ISBN: 0-440-20099-7

Printed in the United States of America
Published simultaneously in Canada

July 1988

10 9   8   7   6   5   4   3   2   1

KRI

This one's for the real experts that the self-appointed "experts" won't listen to, until maybe it's too late. . . .

CHAPTER

1

As he lit his cigarette in the flame of the disposable lighter, he glanced at the Timex on his wrist. It was time to be moving. The cook and the waitress in the stained uniform, who hadn't spoken a single word to him, were still arguing, the cook unseen, his voice like the sound of a hacksaw drawn across metal, the waitress halfway through the kick-splotched dirty yellow swinging door. He tossed seventy-five cents down on the counter for his lukewarm black coffee and walked out, the sounds of the argument inside instantly lost in the honking of horns, the distant wailing of police sirens, and the forced laughter on the street.

It was warm for just after Christmas, even for the deep South.

Everywhere, there were neon lights, flashing, humming, hissing, bathing the faces of overly made-up, pouting-lipped girls in short, tight skirts, and swaggering, sneering boys in wrinkled, baggy trousers. Cars passed, their radios blaring in unending testimony to the Doppler effect, "heavy metal" rising and falling in cacophonous waves.

He stopped beside the alley entrance. Had he been blind, he would have known he'd arrived, the sour smell heavy on the still night air. He looked up and down the street, then turned into the alley, his right hand sliding under his leather-look plastic sport jacket to the butt of the Glock handing in the diagonal black nylon shoulder holster. Halfway down the alley, he saw movement, but he wasn't supposed to see anyone yet, so he kept walking just as if he had seen nothing at all, listening to the sounds of his rubber-soled shoes slap against the slimed alley surface.

"Hey—Johnson!"

Dimitri Mikhailovitch Borsoi turned slowly to his left. "Reefer. How ya doin'?"

"Okay. Thought maybe you wasn't comin'."

"How's that?"

"Well . . ." Reefer apparently didn't know what to say.

Borsoi let him hang a few awkward seconds, then said, "If you and your guys want in, you learn one thing first, Reef."

"Yeah? What's that?" Reefer laughed.

"Always on time. Never early, never late. And that works two ways. If you're on time and the guy you're supposed to meet isn't, clear out. Always."

"Sure—only common sense, man."

Borsoi just nodded, watching Reefer's face in the yellow lamplight for a second longer until he couldn't take it anymore. It was a weak face, made to look strong, even menacing, the fat mouth downturned in perpetual disdain. The mustache above the mouth was thin, with acne pimples showing red on the upper lip beneath it, the hair blond and short at the sides, spiked on top, and with the apparent consistency of greasy barbed wire.

"Everybody waiting?"

"Yeah. I'm the—the reception committee, Mr. Johnson."

"That's a fine idea, Reefer. Always post a sentry just in case something goes bad. There's a lot to cover."

Now the slap-slap sounds of his own shoes echoed in counterpoint against the clicking sounds of the high, hard-heeled gray shoes that looked like a cross between something worn by an affected dandy and a peasant woman from one of the poorer collectives.

They stopped beside the metal fire door, poorly sketched inverted pentagrams and slogans like *Leopards Rule!* drawn over the door's entire surface with various shades of spray paint.

Reefer gave the rather pitiful secret knock, had to give it again, and then the door opened, so wide that all the secret-entry routine would have been for nothing. "Got Johnson with me," Reefer announced as he swaggered inside, Borsoi following him.

Borsoi made a quick head-count. All thirty-four whom he had expected to be there were there, along with a half-dozen slovenly-looking girlfriends in various stages of being mauled by their "old men."

Borsoi walked toward the front of the ground-level apartment, a smell of garbage in here different from the smell in the alley, mingled with dampness and the smell of stale beer. The overhead lights burned, bulbs bare. Reefer, as "gang enforcer," came to stand beside his leader, Smitty. Smitty was tall, lean, but despite the leanness, his muscles rippled at the slightest move. And there was something different about his face, just as much pretend in it, but in the eyes nothing that could conceivably be pretend at all. The eyes showed simultaneous amusement and brutality.

"Mr. Johnson." Smitty stood up and extended his right hand, a studded black band at his wrist.

"Smitty." Borsoi took the proffered hand.

"We made our minds up. How do we earn all this money, huh?" And Smitty laughed. Then Reefer laughed and there was laughter generally for a few seconds. Then Smitty began to speak in an even whisper, all the other sounds in the two dingy rooms dying away except for the dripping of a faucet and the occasional shuffling of a foot. "Mr. Johnson came here tonight to tell us what we do to earn all this money, right? So, shut the fuck up and listen." Smitty looked at Borsoi. "Go for it, man."

"Thanks," Borsoi nodded.

Borsoi turned around to face the rest of them, Smitty and Reefer flanking him. He supposed they were honoring him.

"How many of you are tired of fighting for every damn dime?"

There was some laughter; somebody hooted, "The ones we fight is more tired!"

"Shut up?" Smitty snapped, and the noise died down.

"You don't think about it all the time, because you're used to it. But you're all victims, victims of a society that beat your parents down and beat their parents down and beats you down. You have brains. You have initiative. But you have to steal to use it. I'm offering you a chance to change all that. Nobody'll look down on you

ever again. You won't have to take anybody's shit—
they'll take yours. Money—hell, you'll have more
money than you know what to do with. But better than
that, you'll have the power. Do you want that?"

There were shouts, fists raised and shaken in the nau-
seatingly close air, the ones who had girls with them
grabbing them tighter, some kissing them.

Borsoi looked at Smitty. "We have to talk alone. All
alone, Smitty. Right now."

"That's cool." Smitty lit a cigarette and looked over
his shoulder at Reefer. "Keep an eye on things, Reef."

"Right, man."

Borsoi, Smitty beside him, started back toward the
entrance, hands clapping him on the back, a bottle of
Budweiser shoved into his hand, half of the beer
drained away.

Borsoi inhaled as they stepped into the alley, the sour
smell here better than what was inside. Smitty closed
the door and leaned against it. "Nobody can hear
nothin' through the door. So—now can ya tell me?"

Borsoi splashed the beer onto the alley surface and
tossed the bottle into some collapsed, water-stained
cardboard boxes. "You happy with the government of
the United States?"

"What? What the hell's this shit, man?" Smitty took a
step closer to him. Borsoi's hand edged under his jacket
a little.

"Would it bother you if you worked, got rich, and at
the same time trashed this corrupt government and
helped make a new one, where people like you would
be on top, instead of on the bottom looking up?"

"I don't look up to nobody, Johnson. Shit—what you
sayin'?"

"I'm talking about a People's Revolution, Smitty. It's happening all over this country. You can be a part of it. And not only that, one of the leaders. More wealth and power than you ever dreamed of while it's happening. And after it's happened, you say jump, the people who put you down, the cops, teachers, anybody—they'll ask how high. I'm shootin' you the straight shit, Smitty. That's the offer. Make a new government with you and people who think like you right at the top and make yourself rich along the way. You got a little army in there. They're undisciplined, don't know shit about how to fight anybody besides street punks and lackey cops, don't have weapons that can do a thing. But, if you're willing, that'll all change. You won't just have a couple dozen guys under you, and their squeezes. You'll lead hundreds at first, then thousands. Even your old enemies on the street will flock to follow you."

"You some kinda Communist or what?"

"Does it matter?"

Smitty didn't answer for a moment—thinking about it, Borsoi guessed. So, Borsoi lit another cigarette.

"You shittin' me or not?"

"Not." Borsoi nodded as he exhaled.

"You got other guys like me?"

"Nobody quite like you. But yeah, I got a lot of people in cities all over the United States, guys just as fed up with the government and the cops and everybody crappin' down their throat as you are. You wanna be here—this friggin' alley—smellin' garbage forever?"

Smitty turned and walked a few paces away. His shoulders hunched, straightened. He turned around. "You some kinda nutball or some kinda cop or what are you?"

"A man offering you opportunity. You man enough to take advantage of it?"

Smitty lit up with a torch-flamed cigarette lighter. "If you're some fuckin' cop, you're dead. But if you aren't, then I'm with ya until ya screw me. And then you're dead. You readin' me?"

"I read ya from the start," Borsoi said honestly.

"So—when do we get started, makin' all this damn money?"

Borsoi nodded, threw down his cigarette, and crushed it under his heel. "Your guys are gonna be lookin' for instant gratification. But we give 'em too much, too fast, we'll lose 'em before we really get going. Do you understand what I mean?"

"Yeah." Smitty nodded.

"I've got the perfect thing. We can pull it off if everybody follows directions."

"You make yourself the new head man, Johnson?" Smitty sneered.

"No. That's your job. I'll train you, get assignments to you. After a while you'll be picking assignments on your own. You'll coordinate them with me just in case you need some help or some special equipment. Occasionally the times at which assignments are carried out will be critical. You'll just have to believe me on that. Sometimes a coordinated effort will bring the best results."

"We split the take with you?"

Borsoi shook his head. "No. All I want to do is help you guys to help yourselves. And I want to see this thing come off, this fuckin' government brought down in ruins so something for the people can be built out of it. Do you get me?"

"I get you. You wanna knock off the government in

Washington and everything, and you're usin' us for your army. The Leopards and guys like us. I can dig that. But I'll tell ya, man, I don't give squat about your damn politics. I jus' wanna get what I can grab."

Smitty was one of the smarter ones, and when all of it started coming together, the few like Smitty would have to be eliminated or become even more dangerous. "We're only recruiting fighting gangs, and only fighting gangs with men like you at the top. You'll be surprised how much your people will be capable of once you get into it. And once the thing really gets going, you'll like it. We have contacts that got us all the information on you and the other men like you we've approached, Smitty. I know more about you than you know yourself. Trust me on that. From the first time you got busted to the time in juvenile hall when those six guys—"

"Knock it off!" Smitty snapped.

"Hey. It never goes further than this. All I wanted you to realize was that you're handpicked. We know you're perfect for this. The brains, the guts, the leadership abilities. And the desire. We're usin' you and you're usin' us. That's called a symbiotic relationship, Smitty. And it can work real well."

Smitty lit another cigarette with the torch lighter. "What's this first 'assignment,' like you say?"

"The gun shop a couple blocks from here. Tonight. The cheapie stuff you and your guys can sell on the street and make a bundle. All the people who can't buy a gun legally. You'll clean up easy. And the good stuff— like the AR-15's and things like that. I've already arranged a new headquarters for the Leopards. You can live there if you want. A house a couple miles out of town. Nice and peaceful with plenty of property around it, and nobody to see what you're doing. Bring a woman out there. We even got the lawn care taken care of for you." Borsoi grinned. "And you'll be taught how to convert the AR-15's and other guns into automatic weapons. We have the parts. You can't buy 'em or steal 'em. But we make our own. And then there's something else."

"What? You gonna adopt me?" And Smitty laughed.

"Almost. I took the liberty of having false identification made up for you—Social Security, driver's license, and a gasoline credit card. We set up an account for you under that name. Just outta town. A nice little bank. Clean up, go in there with your passbook and your phony ID. Every month, there'll be another five thousand dollars in there for you. Keep it, spend it, do whatever you want. Just watch yourself that you don't attract attention. And there's no reason to tell anybody else about that—I mean in the Leopards. Just our little secret. Like that other thing."

"You knew I'd go along!"

"If I hadn't known, I wouldn't have asked, Smitty." And Borsoi looked at his watch. "I've arranged things so the best time to hit the gun shop is at eleven-thirty. That's thirty-five minutes from now. We have contacts in the right places. The gun shop has a silent alarm system but nobody'll notice it going off for fifteen minutes. Plenty of time to get in, take what's worth taking, and get out. You'll need your five best men. And Reefer should stay behind to keep the lid on things while you're gone. I came in a pickup truck. Parked down the block. We can use it to haul the stuff away. I'll go along."

"If this is a setup, man—"

"You don't carry a gun. I do." Borsoi ripped the Glock

from the holster beneath his jacket. He shifted it to his left hand as Smitty stepped back, then offered it to him. "Here. I fuck you over, just pull the trigger. That's all you gotta do, Smitty."

Smitty took a hesitant step closer. He threw down his cigarette, then his right hand moved out toward the gun butt. His fingers closed over it.

Borsoi smiled.

He had him.

CHAPTER
2

"Milton Brown's *The Coming Terror* is nothing more than sensationalism of the worst kind," Humphrey Hodges declared, lighting his pipe as he spoke. "He's—he's—the man's full of shit, plain and simple," and he hammered the flat of his hand against the glassy polished surface of the conference table for emphasis.

"How can you say that?" Sheila Lord demanded. She chaired the lecture committee and had sponsored the recommendation that Milton Brown be invited to speak at Thomas Jefferson. And, if it were possible for a black face to blush—and David Holden didn't know for certain that it wasn't—she was blushing now.

Doctor Putnam cleared his throat, which meant of course that everyone should pause because he was about to drop a pearl of wisdom among them. "The purpose of our lecture series is to enlighten and inform both the student body and the surrounding community. Not to cause conflict among the members of this university's faculty. It appears that Mr. Brown's book will neither enlighten nor inform, simply agitate."

David Holden knew he was committing the unpardonable sin. "Doctor Putnam? May I interject something?"

"Certainly, Doctor Holden. Say what you will." Putnam nodded, lighting his pipe.

Holden knew better than to say what he "willed." He thought that the majority of the people around the table with him were behaving like pseudointellectual idiots. "I've read Doctor Brown's book. And I must confess, both from a professional standpoint and from a personal standpoint, I found it excellent. As a historian, I find his premise, however controversial, well founded. As we know, all of us having read *The Coming Terror*"— and Holden looked meaningfully at Doctor Hodges and some of the others who he had deduced from their vague allusions to text, hadn't read it at all—"Brown's thesis is a simple one. I hate to belabor this, but it might help if I stated his thesis, at least as I perceive it." He threw in that because he suspected strongly that Doctor Putnam, dean of the university, hadn't read it either.

"Please, Doctor Holden." Putnam nodded, putting on his best meaningfully pensive expression.

Holden smiled, outwardly and inwardly. He had guessed right. "Well, to be brief, then. Brown's thesis is this: Throughout the world, particularly, to be sure, in the poorer nations, social change is being wrought by violent means. What one man calls terrorism, another calls revolution and another calls civil unrest. But, to paraphrase Mao, all come from the barrel of a gun. In the United States, labor unrest and other socioeconomic manifestations have not led to violence. Indeed, the closest our nation has come to violent revolution was during the upheaval of the sixties. Brown contends that much of this unrest was fomented or at the least abetted by persons acting on behalf of an entire new social order, similar ideologically to revolutionary Communism."

Humphrey Hodges cleared his throat and muttered something unintelligible. Holden continued. "I don't think Doctor Brown's book is telling us to look under our beds at night for Communist conspirators. But what he is saying is that America will, sooner than later, find itself in the same predicament as many other nations. To one degree or another. That terrorism, in the form of a movement to destroy the existing form of government, may well be an inevitability. But, by being informed, and acting on that information, we may be able to blunt much of the effect. He's only talking from a commonsense viewpoint. He has no political axe to grind.

"Brown has been an advisor to various branches of the federal government and to several of our allies, and he's had an ongoing relationship with a good dozen of the top internationally active U.S.-based corporations. In short, gentlemen—and Doctor Lord—the man knows his stuff and would be worth listening to. That's my opinion. And I took the liberty of polling six out of the eight people in my department. All six agreed with my contention that Doctor Brown should be allowed to speak."

Putnam started to speak, but Hodges cut in first. "I have reason to believe that Brown is affiliated with several of the more radical right-wing groups within this country. There's no need to name names; by inviting

Brown here, we're not only inviting trouble and the grave possibility of student unrest, we're also associating ourselves with these radical right-wing groups. And frankly, I don't think Thomas Jefferson University, especially considering the rather ambitious building program we are undertaking, can afford to risk alienating alumni—contributing alumni—at this most critical period. Should one lecturer of dubious credentials be allowed to sabotage this entire university? I ask you that!"

Holden stood up, his hands digging into his trouser pockets. "Humphrey—what the hell's the purpose of using words like *dubious* and *sabotage*?"

"Really, Holden!" Hodges stammered.

"Doctor Brown and his book aside, can't we stick to the issues? What right-wing groups? Maybe you can convince me if you tell me. Come on, Humphrey. You can trust all of us." And Holden's hands swept across the room as he sat down.

There was absolute silence except for the sucking sounds of the two lit pipes, Putnam's a slow, deliberate sound, but Hodges's rapid and erratic.

Then Sheila Lord took out her cigarettes and asked, "Anybody got a light?"

Holden started to rise, but Doctor Putnam, smiling broadly at this break in the silence, fired his pipe lighter and lit her cigarette. "Thanks." She nodded, exhaling the way some women do, blowing a stream of smoke from her mouth toward the ceiling through pursed lips. "I want Doctor Brown to lecture here, on the date we originally discussed. I checked with his literary agent and the date is still open. It seems clear to me that Doctor Holden is of a like mind. I say we have a vote"— and she smiled at Hodges, the third member of the committee who was present, two others never having shown up for the meeting—"family obligations," as Doctor Putnam had explained it.

Putnam cleared his throat. "I believe I can spare the committee the bother of a vote. This meeting is running over and we all have obligations tomorrow, I'm sure. And it has been a very hard week." He put his pipe down on the table, staring at it as if somehow it were undergoing a metamorphosis or getting ready to tap-dance. "I have, in my position as dean, the prerogative of casting a tie-breaking vote or vetoing a committee decision should I feel such a decision merits vetoing. Anticipating the results of a voice vote by the members of the committee present this evening, I feel it my obligation to preempt any voting function since my mind is already made up. I have carefully weighed the facts, the cogent arguments presented both pro and con, enjoyed the liveliness of the debate. But, in the best interests of Thomas Jefferson University, I must ask Doctor Lord to compose a letter on her committee's behalf to the eminent Doctor Milton Brown conveying this university's regrets that, for matters of policy here, we must regretfully cancel the invitation to appear as part of our lecture series."

Holden realized he was staring at Doctor Putnam.

Sheila Lord started to speak.

"My mind is made up, Doctor Lord—and Doctor Holden. And, this meeting is adjourned." Putnam picked up his pipe as he stood, turning away from Sheila Lord and starting away from the table. Holden looked at Humphrey Hodges. Hodges smiled back and shrugged his shoulders. Holden stood up and walked out of the room.

The first-floor corridor of the faculty office building was heavily shadowed, only every other overhead turned on.

He heard the click of Sheila Lord's high heels on the stone floor, heard her saying to him, "I'm sorry David. But thanks for the help."

But he didn't look at her, staring instead at the university crest on the wall outside the conference room doors. The motto of Thomas Jefferson University was engraved there. THROUGH COURAGE, TRUTH.

CHAPTER
3

Rufus Burroughs glanced at his wristwatch as he reached for the microphone. "This is Metro Oscar-November one niner, Sergeant Burroughs. Over."

"Priority for you and Detective Ramirez. Repeat. Priority. You are to report immediately to Deputy Commander Kaminsky. Metro Central Out."

"Roger that, Central. What's up?" Nothing. "I say again, Metro Central. What's up? Over?" Nothing. "Shit!" He threw the microphone down on the seat, leaned across the roof, and spotted Clyde Ramirez coming out of the Burgerland. "Clyde! Yo, Clyde!" And he waved him forward, looking at what was left of his cheeseburger and, suddenly not feeling like eating it, walking toward the swing-lid trash can and pitching it inside.

"What's up, Rufe?"

"We've been pulled off watch," Burroughs told him, wiping his hands on his handkerchief. "God, these burgers are greasy. We gotta find us someplace better to

munch out, Clyde. They want us at Central. Kaminsky
wants to talk to us. I don't know what's up. So, we're off
watch. Come on."

Burroughs slid behind the wheel, Clyde Ramirez
climbing in beside him. "We'll catch a lot of traffic if we
go past Dina-Fab—factory's got a shift change in—"
Rufus Burroughs slowed the car as they hit the driveway out of Burgerland. The warm night, the post-
Christmas holiday season, all of it making traffic heavy
despite the hour—"about ten minutes. We get stuck,
we're on our own overtime, man."

"Hell with that, then." Burroughs took the right instead. "Give us a chance to drive past Hobson's," he told
Clyde Ramirez as he fumbled for his cigarettes.

"You like guns, I don't—but you're as nervous as I am
when you're around Hobson's, Rufe. Somebody cracked
that place, there'd be enough guns on the street to start
a small war."

"You're exaggerating, Clyde." He accelerated on the
amber light and beat the red, kept going. "Bill Hobson's
got some of the best security money can buy."

"Then why you always cruise us past there real slow,
Rufe, huh?" Ramirez laughed.

Burroughs caught himself starting to smile. "Just in
case. Now shut up and eat that cheeseburger before the
smell of the damn thing makes me barf, okay?"

"Okay, already."

Annette would be home by now, he figured. She had
a heavy night at the library, with finals coming up. He
shook his head. Four years of college was all he could
stand. He took the next right down Third.

"What do you think Kaminsky wants?" Ramirez was
talking again.

"Hell if I know, man. Maybe wants to ask our advice on some important administrative matters, huh?" Ramirez started to laugh and then so did Burroughs. Kaminsky was the embodiment of the term *brass hat*. As if idiot-level superior officers hadn't been bad enough those years in Vietnam, he had to get stuck with a bigger idiot on the police force.

Mechanically, without even thinking about it, he was starting to slow up, a block away from Hobson's now. Bill Hobson always gave discounts to the police, but that wasn't why most cops—even the relatively few who didn't much believe in civilian firearms ownership, like Ramirez—liked him. He was a genuinely decent guy. There was never a charity drive that Hobson's Gun and Sport didn't contribute to.

Burroughs found himself smiling again. He remembered a time when he was new on the force and had bought a used M & P .38 from a pawnshop for uniform duty, then found out somebody'd done a home gun-smithing job on it and put the thing so badly out of time, and so completely screwed up the action that the cylinder didn't rotate properly. The pawnshop wouldn't take it back, but offered him twenty dollars for it against a trade on a new one. Out of desperation he had gone to Bill Hobson's. Hobson had looked at the gun, laughed, and said, "Man, did you get screwed. I can fix it, but not without getting a coupla major parts. That'll be four or five days. Should be fine then. Cost about twenty-five bucks or so if I buy the parts right." Looking back on it, he guessed Bill Hobson had read his face. "You don't have twenty-five bucks, right?"

"I got twenty-five bucks, yeah. But, ahh. That's the

only gun I got except a forty-five. They won't let me carry a forty-five on duty."

"Yeah. Thirty-eight Special or nothin' in this town. Beats hell outta me. Hey—tell ya what. You can do me a favor."

"I can do you a favor?"

"Yeah—what's the name, Burroughs?"

"Patrolman Rufus Burroughs."

"Okay, Patrolman Burroughs. I got a brand-new-in-the-box stainless-steel version of this baby, see. And I got a friend who keeps preachin' to high heaven the actions on the stainless guns aren't any good, right? But all it is is the hammer and trigger and all are hard chromed. So just like the blued guns, right? You can help me out. I don't have the time, see, to get into the range there and run a box or so through this so I can speak from authority. I never touch revolvers unless I gotta, so I haven't fired one of these much. But if you fire it, you can tell him what you think. He'll listen to a cop. You a veteran?"

"Yeah. Army."

"Vietnam?"

"I was a first lieutenant."

"See—that's perfect. And in exchange for you helpin' me out, you pay me a dollar so the gun's yours legally and you carry it until this clunker's fixed up. Then sell it back to me for a dollar. You could really help me out, Burroughs."

He'd resented taking charity as a kid, never gotten himself in a position to need it again since that time, but he'd let Bill Hobson loan him the gun. It was either that or not show up for work, and with Annette and school and everything, and both of them holding down full-time jobs, he needed the work.

Hobson's was coming up on the right.

"See! What'd I say before, Rufe. You always slow down."

Every streetlight suddenly went bluish and started to die. "What the hell's goin' on?"

"What the—" Ramirez began.

Burroughs had seen a flash of light from just outside the gunshop as the lights started to go out. He looked up and down the street, the gas station, the twenty-four-hour convenience store. All the lights were out, the darkness total as far up the street as he could see and, as he glanced in the mirror, as far as he could see behind him. He hit the radio. "Oscar November one niner to Metro Central, over."

There was static, which meant that Central either still had power—dubious—or was on emergency power. And everybody was trying to get through, he realized.

"Damn blackout," Ramirez snapped.

"I saw a light outside Hobson's by the side of the building before the lights went out. Let's check it out." He tossed Ramirez the microphone. "You play with the damn radio." He passed the entrance to the parking lot, seeing nothing, then turned into the driveway marked exit only.

He pulled up near the front of the flat-roofed brick building. "You're not goin' prowling around there without backup, Rufe?"

"You try gettin' backup. All I get's static."

"Metro Central, this is Oscar November one niner.

Suspected two-eleven in progress at Hobson's Gun Shop on Third and Cameron. Do you read me, over?"

There was only static.

"Get rid of that useless piece of shit and get the eight seventy outta the trunk, Clyde," Burroughs rasped, sliding out from behind the wheel, the three D-cell Mag-Lite snatched off the dashboard and in his left fist. His right hand pulled the keys and pocketed them, then swept back under his coat to draw the backup gun off his right hip out of the Safariland 28 holster. The department was still .38 Special only, but after a lot of fighting and arguing by people like himself, now allowed use of a backup in any caliber of choice so long as the officer qualified with it. His fist closed on the four-inch Model 629. It wasn't loaded with .44 Magnums, but instead with Federal 240-grain lead hollow point .44 Specials, the shine of stainless steel masked by a black oxide bluing, the oversized factory wood replaced with Pachmayr neoprene grips.

He left the flashlight off. The trunk slammed. He heard Ramirez racking the shotgun.

Burroughs signaled Ramirez as he looked back. Ramirez took the right side of the building, Burroughs taking the left, Ramirez with a flashlight too.

Burroughs did it by the book, approaching the corner of the building with caution, ascertaining as best he could that no one was waiting around the corner, then stepping out, flashlight poised to switch on, supporting his gun-hand wrist, the revolver aimed down the side of the building. Nothing.

He moved quickly, not running though, his revolver tight at his side. He reached the rear of the building. There were no signs of forced entry through any of the windows. And then he heard Ramirez. "Freeze, motherfucker!" He heard the blast of Ramirez's shotgun from the back of the building on the far right side. There were louder cracks, maybe from a .223 rifle, about a half dozen of them. Burroughs turned around and broke into a dead run, made the corner, and crossed the front of the building.

There were more shots now.

He heard the roar of an engine, a black or dark-blue Ford sedan appearing from the right side of the building, and right behind it a pickup truck. Shots came at him from the bed of the pickup, storefront glass shattering, bullets ricocheting off the protective grillwork. Burroughs threw himself into a diving roll toward the doorway, his left shoulder taking the impact—he'd dislocated it in college football and then again in the Army.

Burroughs tracked the bed of the pickup, then fired, double-actioning two rounds as more rifle fire sprayed toward him. He saw his bullets strike, sparks flying off the walls of the truck bed. But he had to pull back. More gunfire, the rear windshield of the police car shattering. Burroughs started to return fire, but the pickup and the car ahead of it were into the street and there was civilian traffic and a miss—"Shit!"

To his feet. Burroughs ran to the car, ripping open Ramirez's door, grabbing up the microphone, depressing the push-to-talk button. "This is Oscar November one niner. Officer down at Third and Cameron. I repeat. Officer down at Third and Cameron. Dispatch paramedics. Over."

Nothing but static. "Dammit!" Burroughs threw down the microphone, running.

He stumbled, caught himself, kept running, reaching

the back of the building, his flashlight buttoning on as he leveled the revolver.

No one was there, except Ramirez.

Still keeping the revolver out ahead of him like a wand to ward off death, he moved toward Ramirez, shone the flashlight all around, then dropped to one knee beside his partner. Ramirez's eyes were closed. Burroughs didn't want to move him. There were at least three bullet wounds across the chest and one more in the abdomen.

"Clyde—hang in there. Ambulance on the way, man," Burroughs lied. He'd seen dying men before. Clyde Ramirez looked like one of them.

"Get—get my head—it's cold, man. . . ."

Gently, Burroughs lifted Ramirez's head. "I'm here, Clyde. Be cool."

"Kids, Rufe—kids—they were. . . ." And Ramirez's head lolled back, his eyes wide open.

Rufus Burroughs licked his lips, felt tears welling up in his eyes.

CHAPTER

4

David Holden was tired of brooding. It didn't accomplish anything and the more he thought about Doctor Putnam and Humphrey Hodges and the rest of the people like them at the university, the angrier he became. He reached out in the darkness and turned on the car radio. Static.

"Hmmph," Holden grunted. He shrugged his shoulders, his left hand on the wheel, his right hand pushing buttons. All of the stations he had the radio set for were nothing but static. "Damn!" He'd never had any problems with the car radio before. He flicked it onto AM, not too many stations available there locally during the evening, most of them smaller stations that only broadcast from sunrise to sunset. But on clear nights like this, despite the distance, he was usually able to pick up that Chicago station that people sometimes got as far away as Canada and Florida. But not tonight.

It had to be the radio.

Despite the clarity of the sky, he couldn't see any

farmhouse lights on either side of the road. He flicked the radio back to AM and tried the dial this time instead of the buttons. Nothing.

Holden reached down for the CB microphone. "Break for channel nineteen. This is Man with Fudd. Anybody out there? Come on back."

There was the crackle of static, then a transmission, a little hard to hear because the guy talked too fast and held the microphone too close to his mouth. "Hey, Man with Fudd. What kinda CB handle is that? Come back."

"I got a Ph.D. in history—you know—a Fudd. Who've I got? Come back."

"This is the Lonesome Lover. Whatcha need?"

"Not that, friend. You got any commercial radio stations coming through? I'm westbound on Three eleven east of Bridgeborough and there's no AM or FM traffic at all. Thought maybe it was my radio. But I don't see any lights from the farms on either side of the road. Usually you can see the chicken houses and the big grain elevator over on Four twelve. Come back."

"That's a big negatory for me, too, Man with Fudd. Just passed the Seventy-six truckstop off the interstate north of you. No lights. Nothin'. Spooky. Got any ideas, Man with Fudd?"

He didn't have any ideas aside from the obvious. "Must be a big power failure affecting the entire grid, Lonesome Lover. You doin' all right?"

"Hard side up and the rubber side down. I'm rollin'. Have a good one. Startin' to lose ya."

"Same here. Talk to you." He left the CB on, the microphone on the seat beside him. He wondered if Elizabeth and the kids had electricity. He doubted it. Bridgeborough had to be part of the same grid. She'd be waiting up for him, like she always did, ready to put together something to eat. But hard pressed for it tonight, he thought. The kitchen stove was electric. But she'd always made do somehow. When he'd asked her to marry him he'd been a college senior with a commitment to the Navy ahead of him and she married him on the kind of money he could earn tutoring, selling a few sketches, and working weekends in Hobson's Gun Shop. Then the Navy, her worrying when he was in Vietnam that he'd get killed while away on some mission, even worrying, he knew, once he was back Stateside on training exercises. The hard part had been being sworn not to tell her anything about the missions or the training.

He had always told Elizabeth everything.

He'd become a SEAL team commander, stayed in six years beyond the four years he'd committed for, then given it up. First came Meg and he realized that staying in the Navy would mean she'd be changing schools every few years. Then David Richard Holden, Jr., Elizabeth insisted on calling him that. But he'd stayed in the Naval Reserves until he had his twenty, retiring with the rank of commander, taking a public information officer slot, every once in a while sneaking out with the SEAL team guys as "research" for his PIO duties.

He finished the graduate program he'd worked on nights while in the Navy; then the professorship at Thomas Jefferson. "Professorship" had translated into "instructor" and it had taken a long time to work out of that, especially since half the guys ahead of him were younger.

Once the professorship came, it meant more prestige but not much more money. Elizabeth had been born into money, but adapted to the lack of it remarkably well. Even in the Navy days, he'd worked, supplementing their income by selling an occasional drawing. He began plying his sideline as an artist in earnest when he started teaching. He'd grown up drawing cowboys and Indians, then, one lucky day, had the inspiration to combine his reading interests in science fiction with his art.

The illustrations he did for magazines, book covers, occasionally for movie posters—though nothing with too big a budget—made up better than a third of their yearly income now.

Dave had the knack for it, but didn't like to draw. Meg liked to draw and, when she worked at it terribly hard, turned out decent work. What she lacked in talent, she made up through determination.

And then, suddenly, there was Irene, named after Elizabeth's maternal grandmother. Irene hadn't been anticipated, but she was no less wanted; maybe because of that she was something special.

Holden's mind drifted back to one of the points in the Milton Brown book. Here he was, driving along a country road at night, and because somebody had hit a transformer or overloaded a circuit, there was no radio, no light. How easily, he thought, the comfortable civilization everyone had become accustomed to in America could be disrupted. And if it were disrupted enough, how long would the fragile infrastructure of freedom under rule of law survive?

He shook his head, wishing the radio worked.

He was tired.

Holden cranked down the window some more. It was almost warm enough for air conditioning. The people who talked about changing climate loved days like this.

December with an afternoon high in the mid-eighties, while other parts of the country were digging out of heavy snows. He started singing—he'd never been much of a singer, everyone told him—"That's What I Like about the South." His Phil Harris impression wasn't that good, either. But he was just old enough to remember radio and he collected cassettes of old radio programs. He could have used one now; at least the tape deck still worked.

The car shuddered slightly. For a second, Holden thought he'd run over something. He cut the wheel right instinctively, almost going onto the shoulder when light and noise came. He hadn't run over anything. An explosion or something, off in the darkness to his left.

"Holy—"

Holden glanced into his rearview. He could see the fireball still rising, already starting to dissipate. He guided the Ford station wagon onto the shoulder and stopped. Reaching down to the CB, he turned to channel nine. "Breaker breaker. Any cops out there? Come back."

"You got the state patrol. We already know there's a massive power failure. Over."

"You know there's been an explosion about five miles east of Bridgeborough on Three eleven, on the south side of the highway?"

"Explosion? Where was that?"

"About five miles east of Bridgeborough on Three eleven. Near that abandoned gas station? I'm going to take a look just in case anyone was hurt."

"You are advised to stay with your vehicle. We're five minutes from the scene."

"I've got some first aid training from the Navy—I'm checking it out."

Holden threw down the microphone and shut off the engine, taking his keys. He started to get out, looked into the darkness. Some brush was burning. The explosion had to have been manmade. He shook his head, leaned across the seat, and opened the glove compartment. He grabbed the MkIV Series '70 Colt out of it, then shut it and turned on his emergency flashers.

Holden got out onto the highway, the .45 going into the waistband of his trousers under his blazer. The first finger of his right hand fumbled the tailgate lock switch and there was a reassuring click. Slamming the driver's side door behind him, he walked to the rear of the vehicle, opened the tailgate, and then opened the larger storage compartment just inside on his left. He pulled out the four-way, the tire inflater, the flashlight. The fire extinguisher. He put the four-way and the inflator back, closed the compartment, put the flashlight and fire extinguisher under his arm, buttoned down the tailgate lock, then slammed it.

No sign of the state patrol guys yet. Holden shrugged. He turned on his flashlight and started walking back toward the site of the explosion.

As he neared it, he could see in better definition what he'd assumed were grass fires before. Even with the power out, apparently enough of a charge was stored in the transformers to cause sparks. Because it was a transformer tower that had blown. He could see that clearly with the brightness of the moon.

He'd read accounts of disgruntled workers taking down telephone or electrical lines as acts of sabotage. But there weren't any strikes on that he was aware of.

He looked up and down the highway again. Still no sign of the police.

Holden put the flashlight under his arm and took out his .45, drawing back the slide, letting it slam forward. It sounded so loud in the stillness out here it was as if someone had dropped a trash-can lid. He raised the thumb safety and put the pistol back in his trousers. He didn't want to get shot by an anxious state patrolman whenever they did arrive.

Holden started walking—slowly—toward the toppled electrical tower. As he neared it crackling sounds became progressively more audible, almost drowning out the crickets. He studied the ground with meticulous care, having no desire to step on a downed power line even if there was a blackout. He hadn't trusted electricity since he was ten years old and had seen the next door neighbor boy killed touching a high tension wire while climbing a utility pole after his kite. Since then he'd seen death in the Navy, but never anything that caused him to shiver just thinking of it. Tommy had just hung there, caught, magnetized by the electricity, his body smoking. And there had been nothing his father or Tommy's father had been able to do.

Holden stopped walking, shining his light over the ground. And he saw something curious. He moved toward it cautiously, dropped into a crouch, and touched it with the muzzle of the flashlight.

He'd seen them, used them. Detonators for plastic explosives.

"Freeze! Twitch and you're dead, boy!"

"Shit," Holden murmured.

CHAPTER

5

"I tried calling the police but I couldn't get anything —I couldn't get a call to go through! David!" She came into his arms and he held her tight, kissed her cheek, found her mouth, kissed her. "Are you all right? I was so—"

"I'm fine. I just had a great lesson in why civilians shouldn't interfere in police work. You and the kids been all right? Any power at all?"

She stayed in his arms as they moved inside the doorway. "The lights went out hours ago. About ten o'clock, I guess. Irene was already on her way to bed and I brought her back down with Dave and Meg and me. When the power wasn't back on by eleven-thirty and you weren't home, I told Meg to take Irene to bed with her and I had Dave and Meg go to sleep. Dave wanted to sit up with me." He could see her smile in the glow of the candlelight. "I convinced them that if anything really were wrong, they might need their sleep. What happened?"

She took his briefcase and set it between two handles on the hall table. "Why's your briefcase so heavy?"

"I put the .45 in it."

"Why?" She started taking his blazer from him. It was cool enough, several windows opened, the curtains blowing, the candles flickering a little in the drafts.

As they walked into the recreation room, he gave her a quick version of seeing the explosion, calling the police on the CB, going off to investigate, getting caught at the scene by the police, and then having to talk his way out of it. The only way he'd escaped being taken in for questioning was by telling them he'd been a Metro cop himself for three years while finishing his Ph.D., then getting one of the state patrol officers to call the patrol post commander. "Remember the guy in my thesis program who used to call with research problems at six o'clock in the morning until I threatened to drop him? That's the state patrol commander's kid. He's got a Ph.D. now and he's working at Harvard. Can you believe that? Probably makin' more money than we do!

"After the patrol commander vouched for me, the cops loosened up a little. Told me that at last count they'd had reports on seventy-four electrical transformers being knocked out here and just over the state line. Thought it was some kind of union thing, but that was just guesswork. The FBI was in on it and everything. I recognized the detonator. It was one of the types we used in Vietnam. Outmoded now, but still effective."

She eased him onto the couch. The rec room looked kind of eerie, he thought, with just candles glowing. But the way Elizabeth kissed him, he deduced that in some way or another she found the whole thing romantic. "Want a drink before all the ice is melted?"

"Yeah—a drink's good."

"You had that I-could-use-a-glass-of-whiskey look in your eye. I can't make you a hot meal. But a sandwich?"

"Got any of that cold Domino's pizza?"

"But I can't heat it up?"

"I like pizzasickles."

"If we don't get the power restored within the next twelve hours or so, everything in the freezer's going to have to be thrown away," she told him, her voice trailing off as she disappeared in the direction of the kitchen.

Seventy-four transformers—just that they knew about—in two states didn't sound like random sabotage. Holden kicked off his shoes and stood up, pulling his tie loose as he walked back into the hallway. He opened his briefcase and took out the .45. He'd already cleared the chamber. He took it back with him into the rec room, set it on the table, opened the cigarette box, and took out a Camel. He'd mostly quit smoking five years ago, but allowed himself a cigarette now and again. This seemed like an appropriate time. His lighter was in his coat pocket, so he picked up one of the candles.

Holden heard ice tinkling and looked behind him. "If the weather weren't so unseasonably warm, we'd have more time on the frozen— What's your gun doing in here, David? Gonna shoot the candles out?"

"That's a thought. But I'm not in practice. Just figured it could—"

"Use a cleaning, sure. Bullshit. You think something's wrong."

He exhaled smoke. Elizabeth dropped to her knees on the other side of the coffee table, taking out a cigarette and lighting it with the same candle, wax dripping onto the table. It was Formica, anyway. She smoked even less than he did these days, but when they'd first gotten married she'd smoked like a chimney. When she'd found out she was pregnant with Meg, that all changed.

"The pizza has to thaw a little, unless you want to eat something four inches thick. Dave put it away. Stacked the pieces one on top of the other."

"Well, let's see." Holden smiled, taking a sip of his drink. "I could take a shower, but the heater's off so there isn't any hot water. I could catch the news to find out what's going on, but the television won't work, and when I checked on the way into the driveway there still weren't any radio stations broadcasting. Gee—I know what we can do."

She smiled. "What?"

"Doesn't require any electricity."

"For most people." She laughed.

"It's healthy—"

"For most people."

"And, best of all—you look good enough to eat and it's either that"—and he stubbed out his cigarette and almost knocked over the candles grabbing for her. She let him and she laughed when he started kissing her—"or eat you!"

"You'll wake up the—*children!*" she half screamed. . . .

David Holden looked at his wristwatch. It was eleven-ten and the sun was shining.

He heard voices coming from the recreation room and then they stopped and then they started again, loud voices. It was that that had awakened him. Holden rolled out of bed, grabbing for the .45 on the nightstand, starting to jack the slide back until he realized what it was.

"The power's back on." Elizabeth yawned.

It was only the television set.

CHAPTER
6

The television news was hard to believe. Contrary to what the police had told him, only thirty power transformers had been toppled by explosion, this nationwide in areas as diverse as their small town in the south and the huge metropolises of Chicago, San Francisco, Los Angeles, Detroit, Dallas, New York City, Atlanta, Miami, and the Washington, D.C., area.

The blackout was widespread because interlocked power grids had been shut down for safety reasons, in the event more towers had been the object of what television labeled "suspected sabotage." "Informed sources" in Washington were quoted as saying there was strong reason to believe some union matter was at the heart of the trouble. The FBI, of course, was investigating. The towers were toppled by charges of dynamite and black powder. No mention was made of sophisticated detonators.

On Saturday, there were no morning newspapers, since presses needed electrical power to turn. The tele-

phone system was still hopelessly mired; all that came
through were strange beeping signals and fragments of
conversations after a wait of ten minutes or more for a
dial tone. David and Elizabeth Holden abandoned any
hope of calling to confirm that Meg still had a scheduled
practice for her dance recital the following week. He
drove her to the dancing school instead, but no one was
there. Lights were on but the doors were locked.

"Why don't we give it five minutes, kid?" he told her,
putting his arm around her as she got back into the front
seat of the station wagon beside him. Her face was a
study in dejection, but a pretty study nonetheless.

"This is really spooky, daddy."

"Well, you'll probably get a call from your dance
teacher tonight or tomorrow and she'll set up a new
time."

"I don't mean that," she said, looking at him. She had
her mother's blue eyes and almost black hair. He imagined legions of boys her approximate age committed
ritual suicide nightly just thinking about her. She gave
him that big smile she'd always used to wrap him
around her little finger. "I mean, well . . ."

"What happened last night scares you a little?"

"I never realized how much stuff you needed electricity for! Like I couldn't wash my hair last night! I
couldn't dry it, couldn't set it. I was going to shave my
legs and even if I could have seen well enough to do it,
that electric shaver you and Mom got me wouldn't have
worked."

"Use a blade," he advised, hugging her close. "Everything's gonna be fine. You heard the news. The FBI's
looking into it. They'll nail the guys."

"I wish Clint Eastwood and Charles Bronson were going after them instead."

He laughed. "Do I detect a note of dislike for these people who gave you a fun-filled night without electricity?"

"When they catch 'em, they oughta lock 'em up in the dark and see how they like it!"

"If McDonald's is running, I'll buy you a Coke, huh? Deal?"

"Deal, Daddy," and she leaned up quickly and kissed him on the cheek. McDonald's was open. There were two short power blackouts in the afternoon, one while they were having the Coke that turned into a milkshake and fries for Meg.

When they got home Dave was out skateboarding. Elizabeth told Holden that Dave was really worried that the local cable station wouldn't have power. *Ben Hur* was scheduled and it was a class assignment for social studies to watch it.

"Where would history have been without Charlton Heston?" Holden commented, opening the special afternoon edition of the morning paper and putting it on the kitchen counter. Elizabeth was making a turkey that smelled good throughout the entire house. "Nothing but the crap they had on the news broadcasts earlier. The guys at the newspapers must have been watching TV too. Why the big dinner? I mean, you know I love turkey, but—"

"I know—what if the electricity goes off, right? If it does before this baby's cooked, Weber kettle time. But, the important thing is if it goes off after it's cooked, we've got all the raw materials for turkey sandwiches. See? Planning ahead."

He nodded, watching her. Irene trotted out of the pantry, decked out in pink shorts and a bib front apron that went down to her ankles. "Got a kiss for me?"

"I'm helping Mommie."

"Mommie always kisses me when she's cooking. See?" He leaned across the counter and Elizabeth stuck her tongue out at him, laughed, then kissed him. He looked down at Irene. "So? How's about it?"

"Well, okay." She let him kiss her. He wondered if Meg was giving her lessons in male manipulation.

The back door slammed. "Dave! Don't slam the door like that!"

"Sorry, Dad."

"He just wants to break the door, that's all," Meg announced as she entered the kitchen. "Let me help you, Mom."

"I'm helping Mommie!"

Meg dropped to her knees in front of Irene. "We can both help Mommie, squirt," and she hugged Irene to her.

Dave said nothing as he entered the room, drawn magnetically, it seemed, to the refrigerator. "Bill Barrow's dad's saying the Communists are behind this. That they're using blacks."

"Bill Barrow's dad didn't call them blacks, did he? And neither did Bill. Right?"

"They're kinda strange," Dave answered dismissively. "You think it was labor unions?"

"No," Holden told his son. "I don't know who it was, but I don't think it was unions. And I don't think the Communists have hired black people to do it either. Maybe Martians." He laughed.

"I was reading this book, you know?" Meg began. She

had the annoying but common habit for girls her age of ending almost every sentence with an upward inflection, as though it were a question, regardless of content.

"A book about Martians?" Elizabeth asked.

"She never read a book in her life," Dave said definitively.

"Buzz off, ant brain," Meg retorted. "But anyway, this book? The country was being invaded?"

"By Martians?" Holden asked.

"No. Communists."

"Ohh," Holden commented, not knowing what else to say.

"Somebody get me the butter out of the refrigerator," Elizabeth commanded.

Dave responded, his other hand filled with a glass of milk. "I'm hungry. Got anything to eat?"

"I'm making a turkey," Elizabeth said quietly.

"But I'm hungry now," Dave persisted.

"Someday your metabolism's gonna change and wham! You'll be as big as the Goodrich blimp," Meg declared.

"Goodyear, dummy," Dave sneered. Holden started to holler about the name calling, but saw the look in Elizabeth's eyes telling him to forget it. "Do you think it's over?" Dave asked suddenly.

"Gut reaction?" Holden asked. "I mean, I don't have any facts upon which to base a truly considered opinion."

"You know what I mean," Dave said.

"Yeah!" Irene chimed in. Holden looked at his little daughter. She grinned up at him.

"What do you think, Daddy?" Meg asked.

"Yeah, Daddy," Elizabeth said.

"Okay. No. I don't think it's over. It was too organized for something casual. You read the Milton Brown book, Liz?"

"I knew you were going to mention that. Yeah. Somebody give me the onion salt," she interjected.

"Onion salt!" Dave exclaimed. "Yuck!"

"I always use onion salt. You just never know it's there. Now listen to your father. Go ahead, David."

Holden began again. "Okay. This book your mom and I both read. This guy Milton Brown is talking about terrorism coming to the United States in the form of a Communist revolution. And what he said made some sense. If terrorism hit the U.S. and it was a clear-cut case of a bunch of Iranians or somebody—"

"Ragheads," Dave supplied.

"Thank you." Holden smiled. "Whatever you call Shiite Moslem extremists. But let's say they were Dave's ragheads, right? Fine. If they did a lot of damage, our government would have to retaliate, right? But, if the terrorists are domestic terrorists, revolutionaries out to topple the government, what do we do? Bomb Pittsburgh? Send out Delta Force—"

"Like in the Chuck Norris movie," Meg enthused.

"Right. But you get the idea? How would the United States cope with the violence? What do you think? Meg."

"Ahh—go after the Communists?"

"Which Communists?" Holden smiled. "Where? How?" And he looked at Dave. "What do you think?"

"Send out guys to infiltrate the revolutionaries and set 'em up."

"Maybe," Holden conceded.

"Me! Me!" Irene shrieked.

Holden looked at her and nodded, trying to keep his expression serious. "Okay, Irene. What would you do?"

"Kick the crap out of 'em!"

"Irene!" Elizabeth exclaimed, her voice a mixture of shock and laughter.

Holden was having second thoughts about the age-old belief that women were peace loving. "What do you think, Liz?" Holden asked his wife.

"Kick the crap out of 'em?" She smiled impishly.

"Ohh, you're a lot of help." He shook his head. "No, see. The only way the government would be able to react would be to cut back on civil liberties in order to hunt down the terrorists. And that would only fuel the terrorist movement. The government would have to become oppressive to deal with the people who said the government was oppressive and that's why they were starting a revolution in the first place."

"Okay," Dave announced. "I get the point. We'd be in deep caca."

"Well put," Holden told his son.

CHAPTER

7

After the Roman fleets suffered heavy casualties during a nearly disastrous engagement with pirates, Judah
Ben Hur had just rescued the patrician commander
Arrius, who would become his benefactor and adopted
father and the key to Ben Hur's revenge. "We interrupt
regularly scheduled programing for this special report.
Live from our news center in New York—"

"What happened to Ben Hur and—"

"The good guy wins in the end," David Holden told
his son. "Liz! Get in here! Quick!"

". . . a night of disaster, suffering, and uncertainty.
More power transformers have been toppled, but loss of
electricity is the least concern to victims and their families in a wave of church, synagogue, and supermarket
bombings, train derailments, and—although possibly
unrelated—a disastrous fire in Pittsburgh at central police headquarters which has claimed lives among police
officers and prisoners as well. The bombings began just
after dusk, in a pattern described by one informed

source who said, 'They've been following the sun. When the sun goes down, they strike. This is bigger than we supposed.'

"How much bigger is it than we had supposed? Heather Richards is standing by live in Los Angeles with this report."

"Holy shit," Elizabeth remarked, Holden just looking at her. She rarely said anything that wouldn't have seemed proper coming from the lips of a nun.

". . . a Jewish synagogue and, across the street, St. Mary of the Angels Catholic Church, both among the most recent targets this evening in a wave of bombings sweeping from East Coast to West Coast. For a live report from New York City, we switch to Harris Wilkes."

"This is Harris Wilkes. Behind me is the gutted hulk of what only a few hours ago was a supermarket packed with holiday-season grocery shoppers: women, children, retired persons, all of them—more than eighty in all, by unconfirmed count—victims of a tragic, senseless bombing. How many more dead and critically injured lie within these ruins is unknown at this hour—"

"Liz—come with me," Holden said, standing up, his wife looking at him oddly. "Dave. Meg. Keep Irene with you and shout when they get to some hard news instead of conjecture. Got me?"

"Right, Dad," Meg called back.

Holden left the recreation room and started up the stairs for the second floor two at a time, the television news reporters' voices droning on, Liz calling after him, "What are you doing?"

"I need a hand."

Holden reached the top of the stairs, rapidly walking

the length of the hall to the closet between Dave's room and Meg's room. He opened the closet door.

"What are you—your guns?"

"You heard what's going on the same as I did," he told her, passing back armfuls of as-yet-this-year unused winter coats, dresses, skirts, and blouses Meg and Liz didn't have room for in their respective closets. He found the twelve-gauge, thirty-inch full Remington 870 and passed it back to her. "Hold this."

"Is it loaded?"

"Shouldn't be, but as I've always told you—"

"Every gun is loaded even if you know otherwise—right. We going to war?"

He found the bolt action .30-06 he used for deer hunting. Now to find some ammo. "Are we going to war, you ask? No—we're already there," he told her.

CHAPTER
8

Christmas break passed. The wave of transformer topplings, bombings, and derailments passed as well. It was conjectured widely in the newspapers and electronic media that a passenger jet which exploded in midair over Nevada was part of the sabotage, but no conclusive evidence had as yet been found and the FAA and FBI were still conducting what promised to be a lengthy investigation. The administration had openly spoken of retaliation against fundamentalist Moslem extremist groups and the Israelis had hit what was described as a terrorist training camp in the Libyan desert. Two Iranian diplomats attached to the United Nations were ordered out of the country.

David Holden turned away from his blackboard list, tossing the chalk in his left palm the way George Raft had flipped fifty-cent pieces, conscious of the gesture because it was imitated by students as a running joke. "So. There's an outline of what happened. The question is: Is it over?"

It had been a more or less rhetorical question but one of the two sophomores in his American Government class raised her hand. "Miss Olmstead—go ahead."

He moved away from the board and perched on a corner of his desk.

"I don't think so, Doctor Holden. Nobody has proven the Iranians or anyone else outside the United States had a hand in what happened. No one has really proved that the events were related."

"That's crazy," Jeff Lyons, a bright but rather abrupt young man, a history major when he wasn't playing war with the ROTC, snapped.

"Mr. Lyons. Apologize to Miss Olmstead."

"But Doctor Holden—"

Holden smiled. "Jeff—it'd be stupid for you to take a failing grade. That'd be crazy."

"I'm sorry," Lyons murmured, clearing his throat so that the words were all but unintelligible.

There was some subdued laughter and Holden held up both hands palms outward to signal silence. "All right. As it happens, though I would have expressed myself differently, Miss Olmstead, I tend to agree more with Mr. Lyons. Miss Olmstead was right, I believe, in her opening statement that the acts of sabotage were not over. But, beyond that, I feel differently. Nothing has been proven, true, but there is a limit to coincidence or synchronicity. Certainly, some of the incidents could have been caused by imitators. You know—'Golly Fred, that sure looked neat, that buildin' burnin' an' all!'—that sort of thing."

There was laughter and he let it subside naturally.

"But I think we have to assume until proven to the contrary that the incidents were organized and accomplished toward the achievement of a purpose. And I'd like you to consider what that purpose might have been." He looked at his wristwatch. "For tomorrow. We've got about forty-five seconds until the period is over. Go have a party or something," and he waved toward the door. As they started moving he raised his voice and added, "And don't forget that section on origins of constitutional government for next time too!"

He turned toward the blackboard, grabbed an eraser, and started removing his outline, the shuffling of feet, the chattering, the laughter, the sudden punctuation of a Thompson chair getting radically realigned when somebody tripped against it, all the sounds so familiar that he was surprised he still noticed them.

"Doctor Holden?"

He turned from the blackboard toward the door. "Annette—hi. Come on in."

Annette Burroughs had been his most promising graduate student, and at the midyear convocation would be receiving a well-earned master's degree. "What's up, Annette? I've gotta boogie, as they say. I mention to you guys that novel I was doing the cover for?"

"The one about space aliens?"

"They're all about space aliens when you bring them down to their lowest common denominator. But, yeah, they like it—but I've got to make a few changes in it between now and tomorrow. So—talk quick." Holden smiled.

She was medium complexioned, her hair a glistening black, styled in what used to be called a "natural," but he wasn't sure if it still was. And when she smiled, the smile lit her whole face. She smiled now. "I'll 'talk quick,' then. You've heard me mention my husband."

Holden thought fast. "The Metro cop? Yeah. I've been trying to recall if I ever met him when I was one, but the name never rings a bell."

Annette Burroughs laughed. "He can't remember you either. I even told him what you look like.

"But anyway, Rufus—that's my husband—asked me to give you an invitation."

"Degree party? I'd love to if I can."

"No—but that too. We just haven't settled on a time yet. This is something different. And it's tonight."

"Listen, Annette; I'd love to. But if I don't have that cover into express mail by tomorrow the art director's going to be really angry. You know what I mean. Art directors waiting for covers can be almost as unreasonable as history professors when they're advising you on your thesis."

Annette Burroughs laughed again, hugging her books to her chest. "Rufus and a bunch of people who were in Vietnam. Black and white. They've got a meeting tonight. Some of them get together every once in a while to shag out old memories and have a few beers. But tonight's a special meeting. Rufus wanted to know if you'd like to come."

"One thing I never do is get involved with veterans' organizations, Annette. Always degenerate into a discussion of what a wonderful time the war was, which is all a crock anyway, if you'll forgive the expression."

"It's not that sort of thing. I've been telling Rufus about you standing up for Doctor Brown's book and wanting him to lecture here. Rufus has read it too. He started reading it the night after the first blackouts. He was the police officer whose partner was killed when that gun shop was robbed. He thinks there's some sort of connection." And she looked around behind her nervously for a second. "He has friends from his old outfit who are cops. Some of them in northern cities, one in Los Angeles. That same night that the gun shop was robbed here, as best Rufus has been able to dig out, at least twenty-eight other gun shops were robbed."

He started to tell her that it was just coincidence, that seizing the opportunity to rob a gun shop which would normally have an alarm system operating was only logical (if you were a thief) when no alarm systems would be working because of a blackout. But then Holden remembered what he'd told Helen Olmstead about stretching coincidence. So, instead, Holden asked, "Has he told the FBI or BATF?"

"They'd know already. Somebody would have assembled statistics like that."

"I suppose you're right." Holden nodded.

"Can you come?"

He started shaking his head. "I really don't have the time, Annette. And a lot of talking about it—"

"Please."

He just looked at her for a moment. "Why's it so important to you?"

Annette smiled again. "I guess I want another voice of reason there besides my own."

"Ahh." He looked back at the blackboard. The question he had spoken aloud and underlined was only partially erased: *Is it over?* Holden turned away from the blackboard. "Okay. Write it down for me. Time, place, any exotic directions. I won't stay long, but I'll come. Okay?"

"Okay." She smiled. "Okay, Doctor Holden."

"Okay."

CHAPTER
9

Rufus Burroughs walked to the middle of the floor, almost directly under the big mirror-faceted ball that rotated as the skaters moved beneath it and reflected the red- and green- and white- and yellow- and purple-colored floodlights located strategically at intervals surrounding the circular floor. He stared out at the faces, a lot of them cop faces that he had invited especially for tonight, guys whose street smarts and overall intellect he respected. And there were his usual veteran buddies, of course.

The two faces that were strangers to him he assumed were Annette's pet professor, David Holden, who was supposed to be an ex-cop, and Holden's wife, whose first name he didn't know. She was one of the prettiest white women he'd ever seen, hair as black as Annette's, parted in the middle and arranged in soft waves to her shoulders. She wore one of those all-weather jackets that looked too big for whoever wore them, and a green-and-yellow plaid skirt.

Mrs. Holden, standing with her arms folded across
her chest, was cold. The skating rink was only used on
weekends and even with the unseasonably warm days,
at night it was damp and in here it was cold. She leaned
against the arena rail beside her husband. Holden was
tall, fit looking, dark-brown wavy hair with a little gray
in it maybe, or maybe it was just the light. Burroughs
had expected Holden would smoke a pipe, but Holden
simply had his hands dug into his pockets and was looking straight back at him.

Burroughs looked down at his feet—public speaking
scared him half to death—and then cleared his throat.
He looked up. "I guess everybody who's gonna make it
is here. So we may as well get started. Most of you know
one another, either friends of mine who were in 'Nam
in my old outfit or some other one or guys I work with
on Metro P.D." He omitted mentioning Holden or his
wife by name. "The reason I asked all you guys to come
—and you ladies too"—Burroughs smiled—"the reason
was that I thought some talking needed to be done
about what went on over the holidays, some talking I'm
not seein' anybody else do. And as a cop and as a veteran, it worries me some of this stuff hasn't been
brought up.

"So, for openers," Burroughs continued, clearing his
throat again, "I've put together some information
which I can't help wondering why we aren't getting
through the newspapers or on television. On the night
of the first blackouts, when Clyde Ramirez got it, God
rest his soul—" there were a couple of subdued amens
from some of the black guys—"on that night, Hobson's
wasn't the only gun shop robbed. From what I've been
able to put together, at least twenty-eight gun shops

were robbed that same night with pretty much the same MO—Method of Operation. All across the country.

"From a couple of my friends, I got some of the poop on what was stolen. Not handguns and stuff you can fence easily, but assault rifles. The semiautomatic kind, but a good gunsmith who doesn't mind breaking the law and can get hold of the right parts—well, we know what he can do, huh? Four of the shops that got hit were class-three dealers. Any of you don't know," Burroughs added, "that means they can inventory selective-fire and full-auto automatic weapons for sale to persons who get the proper licensing after an FBI check and everything. Most of the stuff was collectible stuff, but it could still be used. And that same night, an armory in Seattle —National Guard—was robbed and an undisclosed number of M16's and parts kits were stolen."

Burroughs lit a cigarette, realizing he didn't want to drop ashes on the arena floor, cupping his left palm to catch them. "I did some more checking. There've been three other armory thefts—none of them real big but big enough—and last July, the Spoon River Arsenal was broken into. Aside from an undisclosed number of M16 parts, a set of engineering diagrams was stolen. That'd allow somebody with the right know-how and a good machine shop to crank out all the M16 parts he wanted."

Holden was walking toward him, quickly. Burroughs stopped talking for a moment. Holden was taller than he'd thought, more or less Burroughs's own height of six foot four. "Here." Holden handed him one of the ashtrays from the tables on the other side of the arena rail.

"Thanks, Doctor Holden," Burroughs muttered,

Holden retreating just as quickly as he'd come, moving in a long-strided, effortless-seeming walk. Then Burroughs raised his voice again. "Anybody who follows the FBI reports knows there've been a greater number than normal of bank and savings-and-loan robberies in the last eighteen months. I mean, times are tough for everybody, but you put that and the gun and parts thefts together and on the night of the first blackout there were five more bank robberies. It spells trouble to me. More than we're being told about. And that scares me more. Anybody got anything to say so far?"

Holden raised his hand. "Yeah—Doctor Holden."

Holden took a step forward, hands thrusting into the pockets of the coat he wore, nearly identical to the one his wife had on. "I don't know if this is helpful or not, but that night when we had the first of the blackouts, I was driving home from a faculty meeting and I saw one of the explosions. I got on the CB and called the State Patrol. Just before they arrived, I spotted a detonator on the ground. I was in 'Nam too. It was the kind used with plastic explosives in the early seventies. And when the cops showed up, after I convinced them I wasn't responsible for blowing the transformer, one of the men told me that he'd heard that more than eighty transformers had been brought down here and just across the state line. Didn't match up too well with what Elizabeth and the kids and I heard the next day on the news." He shrugged his massive-looking shoulders and stepped back.

Mike Rothstein, a homicide detective and an ex–Special Forces sergeant in Vietnam, took a step forward. "My sister lives up in Newark. Her husband's a dentist. This one patient of his is some kind of reporter with one of the networks. He tells my brother-in-law that when all the stuff was happening, they had to clear everything they got off the wires with the news director before they could get it on the air. Which is no big deal. But half the stuff, the news director told 'em to kill. This guy —my brother-in-law's patient?—he got pissed and asked how come? Got told it was standard procedure for a national emergency like this."

There were murmured comments, questions, Burroughs raising his voice. "Okay! Hold it down! Anybody else?"

Rose Shepherd, a good street cop who'd just made detective and been assigned to gang intelligence, stepped forward, hands thrust into the pockets of a gray full skirt. She had a pretty voice, he'd always thought. And for the first time, although he'd known her for years, Burroughs realized she had a pretty smile. The smile vanished. There was a gray sweater over her shoulders and every once in a while as she spoke, her hands came out of her pockets to rearrange it.

"A lot of you know me. A lot of you don't. But I work Metro like a lot of the people here. And the oddest thing is that ever since the night of the first blackouts—really maybe a couple of weeks before that—juvenile-originated street crime has been down. Not just a statistical fluctuation—at least I don't think so. But really down. Maybe they're scared. But maybe it's something else too. The Leopards—almost since the very night of the first blackouts—the Leopards have been out of that dump they used as a headquarters and most of the usual stuff they're responsible for has dried up. And it only seems to be the fighting gangs. It's like they all of a sudden retired and moved to the country." She smiled.

There was laughter, somebody cracking, "They should move under the country—six feet of it, huh?"

Rose Shepherd shrugged her shoulders, almost losing her sweater, then stepped back.

"So—what are we gonna do about it, Rufe?" It was Clyde's brother Alberto, neither a cop nor a veteran, but rather a used-car salesman, who asked. "You sayin' some kinda conspiracy or somethin'? That's what caused Clyde to get blown away like that?" The skating rink fell totally silent.

Rufus Burroughs lit another cigarette, looked into the faces looking at him. He hadn't called these people here to tell them he had answers. "I don't know, man. I'd be a liar if I said anything else. But I think we gotta find out. Before we can go to anybody with this, we gotta know more. All of us have friends and relatives that live in other parts of the country, or guys on other departments we can trust, guys who used to be in our old units in 'Nam, like that. I say we call or write and tell 'em a little bit of what we know and maybe find out what they know. Look for a common thread running through the whole thing. Like what if what Rosie said is happening here is happening in other cities. This thing somehow tied to juvenile crime? I mean, we don't know what's goin' on, but we know somethin's goin' on, right?"

There were general grunts and murmurs of agreement, heads nodding, cigarettes being lit. "I say, why don't we do what we can and we get together two weeks from tonight right here if Marty Dzikowski will let us use the rink again? Maybe by then, we'll have some more information and we can get a handle on this thing. Okay?"

There were more nods, grunts, and murmurs and

people started shifting around as if they were getting ready to leave.

Burroughs stubbed out his cigarette and left the center of the rink, friends patting him on the back, making remarks of encouragement, swearing, "There's somethin' up, Rufe—for damn sure," and drifting off. He could see Annette. She was with Rosie Shepherd and Doctor Holden and his pretty wife. He shouldered his way toward them, getting up beside Annette and getting his arm around her waist. "We already met, I guess," Burroughs said to Holden, extending his right hand.

Holden took it, the grip firm and dry and hard, but not a crusher like some guys always tried in order to prove they were tough. He got a feeling suddenly that Holden didn't have to prove anything. "I used to smoke a lot." Holden smiled, letting go of his hand. "I used to get up in front of a group of people and light up and all of a sudden realize I had no place to put the cigarette. I didn't mean to mess you up."

"Hey—no, listen. Thanks. And thanks for chimin' in back there about that detonator thing. You meet Detective Shepherd?"

"I was going to introduce everybody," Annette said, clutching his arm against her. "So—Rose Shepherd, this is Doctor David Holden. This is his wife, Mrs. Holden."

"Elizabeth." Holden's wife smiled, shaking hands with Rosie and then grasping Burroughs's hand briefly.

"Nice to meet you, Detective Shepherd," Holden said, shaking Rosie's hand.

"Rose or Rosie is fine, Doctor. You're Annette's college professor, right?"

Annette laughed. "He's not exactly all mine. He's my

thesis advisor and I really do think he's the best professor at the university."

Holden grinned. "You don't have to say that. I already gave you an A on your thesis."

Annette took his hand for a minute, then looked at Elizabeth Holden. "You have the nicest husband, Mrs. Holden."

Elizabeth Holden gave her husband a hug. "I know. But I try not to say it more than once a week or else he figures he can get away with murder."

"Don't talk about murder in front of a bunch of cops, Liz," Holden told her, his voice sounding dead serious but his brown eyes looking just the opposite.

"You were a cop, I understand," Rufus Burroughs said.

"Yeah. Three years on Metro while I was finishing up my degree. The way Annette talks, I figure we must have missed each other. I was just leaving when you were just coming in. Something like that."

"Were you happy you and your wife came, Doctor Holden?" Annette asked suddenly.

Holden shrugged his shoulders, his high forehead furrowing a little. "I don't know if 'happy' is the right word, but it was interesting."

"Let me ask you flat out then, Doctor Holden. You think there's more to it than we've been gettin' told?" Burroughs watched Holden's face.

Holden ran both hands through his hair and looked him back in the eye. "Yes. But whatever good all of this is going to do, I don't know. If the government doesn't want us knowing about it, hitting them in the face with a bunch of your own intelligence isn't going to make them any happier about giving out all facts. Might just make them bottle up still more. I don't know."

"What kind of outfit you serve with that you were able to recognize a detonator in the dark, Doctor?" Burroughs asked. "If I'm not pryin', I mean."

Holden looked at his wife, his voice low as he said, "See what I mean about talking in front of the cops?" And he looked back at Burroughs. "I was a SEAL team leader. And there was almost enough moon to read by that night."

"I'd like you back at the next meeting, Doctor," Burroughs said.

"I appreciate the invitation. I hope we can make it." And then Holden shot the cuff of his jacket and looked at his watch. "We have to get going. Got a good drive and"—Holden looked at Annette—"I've still got that cover to finish."

"Cover?" Rose Shepherd asked.

Elizabeth Holden spoke. "David's also a professional artist. He paints covers for science fiction novels and does illustrations."

"You remember, Rufe," Annette Burroughs said. "It was two years ago, I think. The university had an exhibition of Doctor Holden's work on display in the fine arts center."

"Boy, did they pick the wrong spot." Holden laughed.

"Oh, nonsense! You're good," Annette insisted.

"All great artists are modest," Elizabeth Holden said, her blue eyes firing with a smile. "At least that's what my husband always tells me!"

CHAPTER
10

It was one of those phone-in programs and once Holden heard the topic, he was tempted to turn the car radio off. "The question then is, 'Do you think more acts of sabotage and terrorism are on the way?' We have a caller on line three. Go ahead; you're on the air."

"Yes. My name is Sandra Wallenski."

"Go ahead, Sandy. Do you think we've got more in store for us?"

"Well, Vic, that's what worries me a lot these days. I mean, if all these terrorists are still out there and the FBI hasn't caught them, they must be planning something, I mean."

Elizabeth's voice was low as she spoke. "I hate to agree with her. But it makes sense to me."

"Don't tell me," Holden groaned.

". . . think they're planning, Sandy? More of the same? More blackouts, more bombings? Are we safe in our homes? I mean—maybe we should be asking that question, too, tonight. Are we safe in our homes with whoever the culprits are still at large. Let me give you the telephone number again so you can speak out and—"

Holden turned off the radio.

"Thank you," Elizabeth almost moaned, leaning her head against his arm. He took his right hand off the steering wheel and put his arm around her, drawing her close. "I knew I should have let the kids get you that 'lover's knob' for the steering wheel." She laughed.

"Who needs it?" Holden whispered, his lips touching her hair.

"You think the kids are okay?" Elizabeth suddenly asked.

They had left the three of them home alone, Meg nominally in charge since she was the oldest.

"Sure," he said noncommittally, gradually increasing pressure on the Ford's accelerator. Elizabeth sat up straighter beside him and shrugged off his arm. He put his right hand on her thigh . . . .

Dave was a natural with the shotgun and Meg wasn't, so Holden had left the shotgun, empty chamber, magazine tube loaded, in the downstairs closet, telling Dave not to touch it unless something happened.

Holden didn't bother putting the car into the garage, both Holden and his wife almost running from the car, up the porch steps, and bursting through the door as soon as he had it unlocked.

Meg hadn't put on the chain or locked the screen door.

But she was in no position for either Holden or his wife to complain about it. Bela Lugosi was charming his

way through another night of the undead, but Meg
wasn't seeing it, sound asleep on the couch.

"Hi, guys," Holden said.

"Daddy! Mommie!" Irene dropped her cards and ran
first into his arms, then Elizabeth's, Elizabeth picking
her up and hugging her, kissing her.

"How was the meeting?" Dave asked, putting down
his cards, too, now.

"Pretty good. Everything go okay here?"

"Oh, yeah," Dave answered almost too casually.

"How come you guys aren't in bed?" Elizabeth
pressed.

"Dave was showing me how to play poker, Mommie!"
Irene enthused.

Holden looked at his son. "Yeah?"

"She's pretty, good really. And it's great for working
with numbers."

Holden leaned over his son and kissed him on the
forehead, his voice low enough that only Dave would
hear him as he spoke, "Get your ass up the stairs, my
friend. Good night."

"Do we have to go to bed?" Irene demanded.

Holden looked at her sternly. "I'll tell you exactly the
same thing I told Dave, young lady. Get your butt up
the stairs."

Dave shouted back, "You didn't say 'butt' to me!"

"Go to bed!" Holden laughed, Elizabeth starting up
with Irene, Holden going over to the couch and dropping to his knees beside Meg. "Hey, kiddo—wake up."

No response.

He shut off the television, realizing he wasn't going to
achieve anything by waking her out of a sound sleep.
He stood up, took off her shoes, and found the woolen

lap robe and put it over her. She twisted around, burrowing deeper into the blanket. He leaned over her and kissed the tip of her nose. "Good night, baby."

She smiled, not awake, and rolled over.

Holden stretched, stiff, no time for a run or for anything to work out the kinks after getting back home today, just a fast dinner and both he and Elizabeth into the car and driving to the meeting, then standing, then driving back.

He took a cigarette out of the box on the coffee table and lit it in the flame of his Zippo. Elizabeth was coming down the steps, her shoes off, the skirt almost down to her ankles. "Want a drink?"

"Sure," Holden told her, following her into the kitchen. She turned on two of the over-the-counter work lights, leaving the overhead off. "I gave up on Meg. She'll be okay on the couch. No sense waking her up."

"Worried about getting that book cover out?"

"I've got time tomorrow morning before class and I can run it over to the post office—"

"I can do that. No problem," she said. Elizabeth poured his glass, then her own. "What's on your mind?" she asked him.

Holden searched around for an ashtray. "I think we should get ready for what might happen," he told her, sitting down at the kitchen table. Elizabeth sat down opposite him, then, her fingers tugging at the bow made out of the collar of her blouse. She undid it, then opened the collar button and reached across the table. Taking the cigarette from his fingers, she dragged on it until the tip glowed almost yellow, then handed it back to him. "What do you think?" Holden asked his wife.

Elizabeth exhaled as she spoke. "You're right, David. But I don't know how we can get ready. Especially since we don't know for what yet."

"By then it'll be too late." They clinked glasses, then sipped their drinks. "If things start happening again, there'll be bans on retail sales of firearms and ammunition. And we don't have the right stuff to defend ourselves."

"That's awfully expensive, isn't it?"

"You got a better idea?" He dragged on the cigarette.

"The money from that cover, if you ever send it out. That'd be enough, wouldn't it, David?"

"That'll be weeks, maybe a month or more by the time everybody up there gets around to signing the check authorization."

Elizabeth's shoulders slumped. "The wallpaper money?"

"No."

"One minute you say this is serious, then the next you say the new wallpaper's more important. What is it?" Elizabeth asked him—playing devil's advocate, he knew.

"You should start carrying that gun I bought you for your purse," Holden told her, changing the subject none too deftly.

"You ever try walking around all day with a purse that has a gun in it? You're talking heavy. If men had to carry purses, boy—"

"I'm serious, babes," Holden told her.

Elizabeth smiled, reached out, and touched his hand. "Okay. But if it's that serious that I have to start carrying a gun around in my purse, what about the wallpaper money?"

Holden looked into her eyes. She was the prettiest woman he'd ever seen in his life. "You've been wanting new wallpaper for the last three years."

"So is it my fault we've got high ceilings and a lot of walls to cover and the only paper I like costs thirty-five dollars a single roll?"

"We could use the book-cover money for the wallpaper," Holden mused. "I mean, if you don't mind putting it off just a little longer?" They had planned to buy the wallpaper and then put it up during the break between semesters.

"You think we should get the things to defend the family right away, don't you? If you needed advice on how to have a baby, I'd expect you to come to me. When I want the definitive opinion on whether or not the family's going to be safe or not, I go to you."

"We're talkin' heavy-duty money, Liz."

"I'd rather have my family alive than have new wallpaper for an empty house," she told him flatly.

Holden offered her the cigarette—she shook her head—and then took a last drag on it himself before stubbing it out. "You can't cut corners on something like this."

"I know that. When we get the wallpaper, I won't cut corners either. Okay?"

"Okay," Holden told her.

"So—what horrible implements of war will you buy?" Elizabeth smiled, leaning across the table and lowering her voice to a conspiratorial whisper. "Rocket launchers? One of those fancy bow and arrows like Sylvester Stallone used?"

Holden gently put his hand over her face and shoved her away. "Right."

CHAPTER

11

Holden had called Jack Crain as soon as the time-zone difference made it nine A.M. in Weatherford, Texas. When Holden had been in the SEALs, he had carried a wide range of knives, never finding one that had perfectly suited his needs. He had met Jack Crain at a science fiction/fantasy convention and the two of them had hit it off instantly. Holden had sketched out a rough idea of what he thought the perfect fighting/survival knife should be, the custom-knife maker changing this detail and that, the two of them finally arriving on what both felt would be ideal for serious utility both in battle and day-to-day cutting chores, yet concealable if necessary.

"Jack. This is David Holden. I don't know if you remember me or not—"

"Sure I do. I'd been meaning to call you up and visit a little. So, how have things been, David?"

"When you get past the blackouts and everything?"

Crain laughed. "Well, I don't know what to expect next. How's your lovely wife and the children?"

"Ohh, they're just fine. Listen, ahh—remember that knife we designed on that cocktail napkin?" Holden felt stupid even mentioning it.

"As a matter of fact, I do. That's why I was gonna call you."

"Yeah? What about it?" Holden asked.

"Well, I got the bug in me the other evening, you know, and after dinner I went down to the shop. There was still something that just wasn't right about it. The knife we were talking about. But the design intrigued me so much, I decided to make one up anyway. So, I changed the blade shape just a little. I made the spine so it could be sharpened just in case you needed a true double edge. And I thought it could use a hollow-ground look, but I still wanted a flat grind. And I found this great new synthetic handle-material. I wound the actual handle with rope first, you see, then applied this new material over it. I made this one with a hollow handle like we talked about, but I figure it'd make a nice full-tang design too. If I do say so myself, it came out really nice."

"Could I get that one? The one you made up the other night?"

"Well, I reckon. But then I'd have to make one up for me. Tell you what, David. I'll send you out this one and make up one of the full-tang models for me." They talked longer and in the end—for a price Holden considered more than fair—Jack had promised to get the knife out to him by express.

Then Holden called Hobson's gun shop and spoke

with Fred Albright, who generally ran the shop these days. "Fred. David Holden. How you doing?"

"David. Boy, you been a stranger lately!"

"Been saving my money so I haven't been shooting too much. But I need to buy a few guns. Any discounts for ex-employees?"

"Maybe." Albright laughed. "Depends on what you want to buy."

"You guys make out all right after the robbery?"

"They didn't do much damage. It was a professional job if you ask me, just large-capacity nine millimeters as far as handguns go and anything that could conceivably be considered a civilian legal semiautomatic assault rifle, and then all the nine millimeter, two twenty-three, and three oh eight they could carry. We were insured, but it still hurt."

"How's Hobson?"

"Broke his foot tryin' to ski again up there in the mountains, but he's okay. Complains as much as ever."

"Look. Here's what I need. I need an H and K ninety-one—the three oh eight?"

"All right. I got two comin' in and only one's spoken for."

"I want four twenty-round magazines and those things they used to call 'jungle clips' to keep two magazines together. Know what I mean?"

"I've got those and the mags, David."

"A cleaning kit and a sight adjustment tool."

"Let me write all this down," Albright said. "Hang on —damn pencil's broken and the pen's outa ink." The receiver went down with a clunk, but in a second Albright was back. "Shoot, if you'll pardon the expression."

"You got any of the Beretta ninety-two Fs, the new military pistol?"

"Yeah—I've got exactly one. And I also have one of the little ninety-two F compacts. Scarce as friends at a bankruptcy hearing." He laughed.

Holden made a decision on the spot. "Both of them—the full-sized and the compact. Give them to me. How about spare magazines?"

"How many?"

"Eight?

"Including the ones in the boxes?"

"Eight full-size. You got them?"

"No. But a dealer friend of mine north of here does. I think. You want any of the twenty-rounders for the ninety-three R?"

"Two. If you can. Do I owe you my oldest child yet?"

"Meg? Well, she's a beauty all right. Maybe a second mortgage would be better, though."

"We'll see," Holden told him. Albright agreed to work out a little bit of a volume discount for him by giving him the accessories at cost. Holden countered by asking what kind of price he could get on the web gear and ammunition he needed and Albright did right by him that way too. A police shotgun would have been good, but the budget was stretched already and the sporting pump he had could be used in a pinch by pulling the magazine plug and, if necessary, hacksawing the beautifully blued barrel back to just at or over eighteen inches. Paramount in Holden's thinking was that he not violate the law in any way. He somehow felt that could prove as critical as being inadequately equipped.

He made arrangements to go in and pick up one of

the two Berettas that afternoon so he could pick up the second one later, when he purchased the rifle, obviating the additional paperwork that would be required of the gun shop for a multiple handgun purchase.

While at the gun shop, he purchased a shoulder holster for the Beretta. Holsters were something he had discussed with Jack Crain and he made a second call to Crain, asking that the Texas knife-maker arrange with the factory to have one of their optional inverted knife sheaths made to accommodate the custom knife. And, Crain agreed to do so.

On the news that night, there was talk of possibly rising oil prices, the low inflation rate, and some sort of Washington scandal. But there was no real news at all.

Holden and his son cleared away the dinner dishes, Meg and Irene emptying the dishwasher while Elizabeth cut the pie she and Irene had made that afternoon. "I ordered the things we need, for the most part. That package I brought home is one of the Beretta pistols."

"Like James Bond, right?" Meg chimed in, then lowered her voice and tried to make herself sound British. "That damned Beretta again!"

"Meg!" Elizabeth interjected.

"Meg said a bad word!" Irene laughed.

"Try carrying on a serious conversation around here, right Dad?" Dave remarked.

Holden just looked at his son, nodding his head. "The rifle and some of the other stuff should be in soon. When we go in for that, I'll pick up the second pistol."

"Two?" Elizabeth asked, laying a piece of apple pie onto a dessert dish.

"He had them and I figured we could use them," Holden said, trying to keep a defensive edge out of his

voice. "Your mom and I've been giving this some serious thought," Holden began again, sitting down, Meg
helping her mother put out the pie, Dave getting ice
cream out of the refrigerator's freezer, Irene snuggling.
"Over the semester break—"

"I wish we got a semester break," Meg interrupted.

"Don't interrupt your father," Elizabeth scolded.

"I wish you guys got a semester break, too, sweetheart. But over the break your mother and I are going
to get really familiar with these new guns, and on the
weekends you guys are going out with us. Dave—you're
pretty good with a shotgun already, but I want you to
get better. And Meg. You're going to learn a little more
too. Same for both of you with that bolt-action rifle of
mine. I want both of you to learn how to handle it. Your
mother shoots okay already with it. So it's up to both of
you guys to improve."

"What about me, Daddy?"

Holden looked down at Irene, then at Elizabeth, then
back at Irene. "Tell you what, babes. That twenty-two
rifle I've got? Teach you how to shoot that if you prom-
ise me never to touch it unless one or the other of us is
around and helping you. Okay?"

"Sure!"

"Okay," Holden told her, kissing her on the forehead.
"Now. We don't have an unlimited budget for ammo
like they do in the movies, but we'll have plenty of
ammunition for everybody to learn to handle at least
two weapons competently."

"You really think it's gonna get to that, Daddy?" Meg
asked, sitting down opposite him.

"I have this uncomfortable feeling, sweetheart, that
yeah—it's really going to get to that. And if we aren't

prepared to take care of ourselves until help comes or
whatever, we're going to really regret it. Trust me on
this?"

"Sure I do," Meg smiled.

"Can I try the assault rifle, Dad?" Dave asked, holding his mother's chair for her, then sitting down himself.

"Sure you can. And I want you to get good at it. And
Meg. The pistols are for you too."

"I'll like the pistols better," Meg declared. "Rifles are
so heavy."

"Girls!" Dave observed.

"Some of the toughest guerilla fighters in the world
have been women, my man," Holden reminded his son.

Meg stuck her tongue out at her brother, then
laughed.

"Do you think you can teach us to be good enough?"
Elizabeth asked suddenly. "I mean, you had all those
years of training in the Navy and then three years as a
policeman. How good can you train us to be in a short
time?"

He caught the tone of the question; or rather, not so
much her question at all as her trying to put into words
the unspoken doubts of the children.

But he answered the question as though it were hers
alone. "We don't have much choice, Liz. We saw what a
brief disruption of electrical power did to affect our
world. Imagine if the electricity were down for a week.
Imagine the telephone service being as jammed up as it
was for a week or better. How would we get help if we
needed it? At least we have the CB radio in the station
wagon. But what if the police couldn't come for a while?
What if we all had to become instantly self-reliant? I
guess that's what I'm talking about with this. We have to

learn how to take care of ourselves. I purchased the best equipment available that was legal to own. So the rest of it is up to us. And it should be fun, learning new things, getting better at old things. Right?"

He was looking for enthusiasm from the children, Meg especially, but at least he felt he had their cooperation.

Elizabeth said, "Who wants ice cream?" And, naturally enough, Irene was the first to respond in the affirmative. . . .

The Jack Crain knife arrived by the end of the week and with it the specially built knife sheath that worked with the shoulder holster, a note from Jack inside saying that he hoped Holden liked it.

Holden more than liked it.

The knife's blade was a modified English Bowie pattern with sharpened recurved edge, the spine indeed left dull but ready to be sharpened. Of stainless steel, the barstock was a quarter inch thick, the hollow-looking flat-grind blade polished mirror bright, the very slightly upswept point as dead true to the blade's center line as a spearpoint. Length from the contoured fully circumferencing guard to the tip was seven and seven-eighths inches, the sides of the guard polished bright, the guard otherwise matte.

The conical butt cap, knurled where it met the handle, was shaped for use as a skull crusher rather than a hammer. The hollow handle, machined out of a solid cylinder of stainless steel, then mated to the blade tang, was adequately capacious for survival necessities and the spare parts he had ordered for the Berettas—extractor, firing pin, firing-pin spring. Length overall from buttcap to point was thirteen and one-half inches.

Engraved along the right blade flat at the top just below the spine was a a single word, DEFENDER.

CHAPTER

12

Partially against his better judgment, David Holden decided to attend the next meeting of Rufus Burroughs's veteran's group. There were more police there, this time, the skating rink twice as crowded (or seemingly so) as the last time.

Elizabeth had stayed home with the children. Both Dave and Meg needed help studying for tests the next day, and Irene was just getting over a brief head-cold. It was the quiet that had kept her home, too, he knew. The official quiet bred uncertainty. Except for an occasional reference, the terrorist acts over the holiday season had faded from the news. Life went on as before. But what had happened to the people who had committed the acts of sabotage and mass murder? That question remained unanswered and Holden had little hope that the meeting would provide any fresh insights.

He watched Burroughs and listened. Burroughs was about six four, Holden's own height more or less, a craggy-faced man whose skin was several shades darker than his wife's, his hair close cropped and showing just a little gray, his chest and shoulders broad, and, the way his neck and shoulders were set, it was obvious Burroughs was a body builder. Burroughs's voice was only slightly southern accented as he spoke.

"The best information I can get is that there has been no official connection made between the sabotage of the power transformers and the derailments and the bombings and all of those gun-shop and bank robberies. I caught the news tonight on the car radio and there's talk of a congressional committee to investigate the bombings. So maybe they'll make the connection. I don't know. I do know, as far as my friends can tell me and as far as stolen-property reports go, none of the weapons have been found that were stolen that night—unless the government's being really quiet about it."

Holden raised his hand.

"Doctor Holden—yeah?"

"Any of those arsenal robberies you mentioned—were plastic explosives or any other types of explosives taken? And how about detonators like that one I saw?"

"I'm glad you asked that, Doctor. I decided to do some checking with the state cops. I found a copy of the report concerning you calling in that explosion, and some routine information and how they let you go and everything. There's no mention of a detonator of any type being found. I checked to see if there was another copy of the report, maybe a classified version. Best I could learn, there wasn't.

"So," Burroughs went on, "I checked with one of the officers who signed the report. I asked him if anything peculiar had been found at the site by them or the FBI. Now, I've known this guy on and off for the last six or seven years. He tells me it's none of my business and walks away. Somethin' isn't right."

Holden admired men with a talent for stating the obvious. . . .

It had been a spur-of-the-moment thing. With all the preparations for commencement, being told at the last minute he was making a speech, all of it, he had needed to unwind. And he had just picked up the rifle and the rest of the things he'd ordered.

After dinner, he dialed Rufus Burroughs.

"Sergeant Burroughs? This is David Holden."

"Yeah, how you doin' Doctor. My God, is Annette nervous. Were you this nervous when you got your master's degree?"

"Not really. But I was scared shitless when I got my doctorate that they'd realize they'd made some kind of mistake and I wasn't really going to get it. She'll be fine. Your wife's a bright lady."

"Thanks. What can I do you for?"

"Commencement isn't until eleven. I wanted to see if you had any plans for tomorrow morning. I guess you probably do, but I was thinking about doing a little shooting. Wanted to see if you might like to come along. There's a good spot a friend of mine lets me use that's about twenty minutes' drive from the campus."

There was a little silence. then, "Sure—wait a minute." The phone went down, Holden hearing some unintelligible conversation in the background, then, "Annette said she'd be happy to get me outta here. Where you wanna meet?"

"Hang on," Holden told him, putting down the phone. "Hey, Liz?"

His wife called back from the kitchen. "What, David?"

"Could Annette Burroughs pick up you and the kids tomorrow before commencement?"

"Sure. You and Sergeant Burroughs going shooting?"

"Yeah—you sure it's no problem?"

"If it's no problem for her."

Holden picked up the receiver. "Tell you what. Why don't I pick you up and could Annette pick up my wife and kids?"

"Don't see why not; that way, we don't have any car shuffling to do afterward. You comin' to the party?"

"Yeah. Thanks for asking us."

"No sweat. What time, Doctor?"

"It's David. How about eight?"

"Sounds good, David. See you then."

Holden hung up. "Hey, Dad?"

He looked toward the kitchen. "What's up, Dave?"

"One of the trucks on my skateboard's loose. Give me a hand?"

Holden had to think for a second—trucks? The thing that the wheels were attached to. "You bet."

CHAPTER

13

Later, at the range, David Holden watched Rufus Burroughs opening his gun cases. "I give. What's that monstrosity?"

"This?" And Burroughs held up a black-finished semiautomatic pistol that seemed huge. "It's a Desert Eagle forty-four Mag. Terrific gun. Fires regular forty-four Mag ammo like you'd use in a revolver, see," and he produced a box of Federal 180-grain jacketed hollowpoint .44 Magnums. "But, it's a semiauto. Works great so long as you remember to clean it every hundred and fifty to two hundred rounds. They recommend heavier bullet weights, but this hundred-eighty-grain Federal works fine in my gun, so that's all I use. Try it."

He buttoned out a massive-looking magazine and started stoking it, the revolver cartridges looking impossibly large. "Here—get the full effect." Burroughs grinned. He opened something that looked like a 1950s gym bag and took a black fabric SAS-style holster from it. "Know how to use one of these?"

"Yeah." Holden nodded. He looked at the label. It read SOUTHWIND SANCTIONS. Holden secured the holster to the belt of his blue jeans just by opening the Fastex-style buckle, sliding one piece under and over his belt and closing it. There were two leg straps rather than one, a good idea, Holden thought. He secured both around his right thigh. The holster had a spare magazine pouch but that was empty. "I like this holster."

"Me too," Burroughs said. He proceeded to show Holden how the Desert Eagle's safety worked, giving him a quick general familiarization.

"Now—this'll rip my arm off, right?"

"You fire a regular forty-four revolver?"

"A buddy of mine's got one. You notice them when they go off, but it never knocked me on my ass, or broke my wrist."

"Try this." Burroughs grinned.

Holden holstered the Desert Eagle, put his muffs up, and then took the pistol in his hand again. Burroughs had his muffs up.

Holden picked a target of opportunity—a pine cone on the embankment fifty feet away that served as the backstop—and thumb-cocked the hammer. He took a good, solid two-hand-hold and fired.

There was a blazing cone of muzzle flash—the morning was overcast—but recoil was absurdly mild. The pine cone disintegrated. "This is like shooting a forty-five with hardball."

"Yeah. Isn't it wonderful, David?"

"You, ahh—you mind?"

"No—take the other seven, have fun."

David Holden did just that, the Desert Eagle faultlessly popping off the remaining seven rounds, accurate too. "This is terrific!" Holden exclaimed, pulling off his muffs, leaving the gun action open after the last shot.

"I'm talkin' some of the SWAT team boys into trying them. For special purpose use, you can't beat it. I shot this baby through both sides of a full-sized American car using the same ammo. For some barricade situations when you know it's only the subject hiding out or when you need a very definite fast one-shot stop, this could be a lifesaver."

"I like it. I really do." He wished he hadn't just spent all his money, but mentally shrugged.

They swapped off, firing their own guns and each other's, Burroughs apparently dedicated to the .44 Magnum, dumping the duty .44 Specials out of the cylinder of his revolver and firing the same loads used in the Desert Eagle. Holden found himself impressed with the out-of-the-box Berettas, their accuracy being more than acceptable and, even in rapid fire, functioning flawlessly.

Holden took out his shoulder holster and put it on. Elizabeth had helped him to adjust it for proper fit the previous evening. With the various safety systems applied, Holden was confident the gun wouldn't dislodge no matter what he did; no matter what the body position or activity, the gun seemed equally secure. On the off-gun side, the inverted double magazine pouches accommodated either standard or twenty-round-length magazines. The sheath for the Defender knife rode inverted as well, the sheath reinforced with metal at the tip to prevent the knife punching through into the armpit, and the knife held into the leather by means of

safety straps. Holden was confident the sheath would
hold the knife securely.

Burroughs commented, "I like that shoulder rig. Hol-
low-handle knife?" Holden showed it to him. "You
could carry a few necessities in here, maybe a few spare
parts."

"Open it."

Rufus Burroughs unscrewed the buttcap, pouring the
individually packaged contents into his left palm. A
spare firing pin, firing-pin spring, and extractor for the
Berettas, the same parts usable in either gun. Matches,
water purification tablets, and a few other necessities.

"Slip your holster on and you're ready for anything
with those twenty-round magazines. You're thinkin' the
same way I am, aren't you? The war's comin' home.
Trouble-in-River-City time, right?"

"You read Milton Brown's book. Your wife told me,"
Holden said. "I think what happened was a test, to see
how we'd react to mass incidents, see who we'd blame,
see how fast we could bounce back under optimum
conditions."

"I've been talkin' with a few of my friends. Only
people I can really trust. Can I trust you to keep this just
between us, David?"

"All right, Rufus. I suppose you can," Holden told
him, his voice low.

"We're thinking about forming a little organization of
our own. Cops and veterans mostly. You'd be eligible
either way. I checked on you behind your back. I'm
sorry, but it was the only way I could be sure on that
detonator thing, after that guy I'd known all those years
clammed up. You did some pretty hairy stuff in the
SEALs, and that's just the unclassified stuff."

"What are you planning, Rufus?"

"We're putting together a little network, to provide us with intelligence and an organization we can utilize in the event the pizza hits the fan and things start fallin' apart, things the government can't or won't handle."

"That's not the way to do this, Rufus. Look—I mean, I respect your intentions. But things like this never work. No matter how good you start, it turns into vigilantism. Even good guys with training and discipline will go wrong. Thanks for asking me. But don't tell me any more about it, okay?"

Burroughs's eyes hardened for a moment, then he smiled. "Okay. I respect people bein' up front. I think you're wrong and, worse, I think you're gonna find out you're wrong. So, consider the invitation still open when you need it."

"Thank you," Holden said honestly.

Holden looked at his wristwatch. It was nearly time for them to leave. He started shrugging out of the shoulder rig. "When are you gonna start wearin' that thing all the time?"

"Not until I need to," Holden told him. The wind was picking up a little. If it intensified, it would play havoc with the microphones and the speaker system during commencement. "This is analogous to fire insurance, Rufus. When you get it, you don't sit around waiting for the house to burn down, but it's comforting to know you've got it to fall back on just in case."

Burroughs was reloading his revolver. And then Burroughs smiled. "But with fire insurance, David, you don't have to carry the policy around with you, just remember the name of the company and if something happens, you're covered. Won't help you a bit, when push comes to shove, for you to shout 'Beretta' in some-body's face, will it?"

David Holden didn't answer him.

CHAPTER
14

Elizabeth Holden sat perched on a corner of David Holden's desk, the desk uncharacteristically clean because classes were now, officially, between terms. Lines of light cut across her face and her body through the slats of the Venetian blinds; the gray smoke from the cigarette held casually between the first and second finger of her right hand curled upward, becoming gradually opaque. Elizabeth looked very sexy, Holden thought. She wore a black sheath dress with high round neck and long sleeves; white pearls at her throat, small white pearl earrings, and the gold lady's Rolex her parents had given her (which she only wore for special occasions) were her only jewelry. Her black hair was up, wisps of curls flirting with some otherwise unnoticed air current there at the nape of her neck. Her long legs were crossed, the dress up to her thighs, one of her high heeled shoes half off as she swung her right leg a little provocatively. "You look like the sexy client in some private-eye novel," he told her as he took off his boots.

"I'm waiting until you get down to your underpants, then I'm going to scream, 'Rape!' and just sit back and laugh," she told him. "There is an advantage," she began again, apparently changing the subject, "to having a husband who only wears black, brown, or blue ties. He tells you to bring his good blue suit and you know exactly which tie to bring along."

"I wanted the brown tie. It goes better with my white socks," he said, pointing at his feet. He started to get out of his Levi's. "Meg and Dave keeping a good eye on Irene? I remember the last time she came to commencement. It was like a Chinese fire drill."

"She's much more grown up now. Very ladylike. She's wearing her white gloves. And her Easter hat from last year. She looks cute."

"Takes after her mother."

"I won't argue with a compliment, but she looks more like you. Except being a girl and all."

Holden stared at Elizabeth for a second.

"I mean," Elizabeth went on, "she's gentler featured, but she has your coloring, your bone structure."

"Poor kid."

Elizabeth laughed. "No—she's beautiful. You're handsome. Especially now that you're down to your underpants."

"Toss me my pants."

"Maybe—maybe not," she answered. "Anyway, change socks first. Let me keep you guessing for a while." And she shifted the cigarette to her left hand, taking up the ball that was a pair of blue socks and holding it limp-wristedly for a moment. Then she flipped it to him and he caught it. "I always liked playing catch with you."

"Keep looking at me like that and you'll be playing snatch with me instead. The hell with the graduation."

"Maybe I won't give you your pants." She smiled evilly.

"'You say it, but you don't mean it,' to quote the Bickersons." Holden laughed. He sat down on the desk chair he'd moved over into the corner of the office and changed socks.

"Got your speech all ready, David?"

"Pretty much. You know me. A few notes and I wing it."

"Annette Burroughs's party sounds like fun."

"Yeah—we should have a good time."

"You and Rufus Burroughs have a good time being macho with your guns?"

"You always have a good time when you're macho," Holden told her categorically.

"Hmm. Show me?"

Holden stood up, his socks on anyway, and walked over to the desk, his arms folding around her. He kissed her hard on the mouth, feeling her hands going into his hair. Breathlessly Elizabeth whispered, "Wouldn't it be neat if Dean Putnam walked in right now?"

"Or Humphrey Hodges."

"No—he might try jumping your bones for himself." She giggled. He kissed her again. She patted his rear end. He grabbed her and kissed her harder this time. "Now I guess I will have to give you your pants," and she looked down toward his crotch. He didn't have to look down himself to know what she meant. He took his pants, stepped into them, and pulled the zipper halfway up while he started into his shirt. "When we get home, why don't we call for a pizza and let the kids watch something on television?"

"Want me to crack open that bottle of champagne?" Holden asked.

She seemed to consider that a moment, then said, "Yeah! Why not?"

"Okay."

He started knotting the knit tie at half mast, not intending to pull if all the way up until the last minute. He sometimes thought that was the reason he'd gotten out of the civilized Navy—just to avoid wearing a necktie. . . .

The sun shone brightly and the wind had dropped to a faint but stimulating whisper.

David Holden stood up as he was introduced by Dean Putnam. Putnam shook his hand, winking and saying under his breath as he closed his left palm over the microphone, "I knew what you'd talk about, David. We didn't need Milton Brown coming to speak. Give 'em hell."

Holden stared at Putnam, dumbfounded.

Putnam let loose his hand.

Holden stood before the microphone, reaching into his pocket for the note cards, realizing they were useless now, really. He began with the usual litanizing of the dignitaries present, then said, "When I was asked to speak, it came as an unexpected honor. So many of those graduating today or receiving advanced degrees are young men and women whom I have come to know and respect for the future leaders in their chosen professions which they will assuredly become.

"One becomes used to the 'captive audience' of the

classroom or lecture hall, and, at the outset at least, addressing such a distinguished body—especially one where most of those present can yawn if they like or just get up and leave—is a bit intimidating at first thought. But it is also an opportunity. The senior class valedictory speech touched on an important issue. The issue was, of course, understanding what has gone before in order to prepare for what will come tomorrow. But another aspect of that same thesis is this: understanding what is occurring now in order to survive the next instant.

"As an historian, of course, I deal in matters which can be judged through the all-pervading wisdom of hindsight. But, when trying to understand the here and the now, sad to say historians are just as much at a disadvantage as the rest of the world. We look, we evaluate, we attempt to base an understanding of the now on what has gone before.

"So, indulge me then for a few moments as I attempt to interpret the here and now." Holden could see Elizabeth's face—she was smiling almost too much, as if telling him, "Go for it—I'll love you even when you lose your job." Irene—beautiful Irene—was fidgeting, but in a ladylike manner, of course, with her white gloves and her Easter hat from last year. Dave—honest man always —looked bored to death and not nearly so comfortable in blue blazer and gray slacks as he did in shorts or half-destroyed Levi's. And Meg. Her hair was up, like her mother's. She looked the perfect lady, the perfect beauty. And she was smiling at him too.

"Like most of you here, I have a family. I love them a great deal, and I look to the here and now and have serious trepidations." He focused on Elizabeth, on the smile he saw. "This nation has recently undergone serious trauma, but that is not what I wish to address. What bothers me more than the possibility that the violence of the holiday season will be repeated is the apparent reluctance on the part of our government to tell us what is happening."

He heard engine noises, like vehicles overrevving.

Holden looked up.

Faces in the crowd were turning.

Holden looked out across the commons.

A green van. Coming up the walkway at the center of the commons. Another van—gray—behind it. A blue, four-door sedan, the left front fender all but crushed. It was behind the gray van.

Holden stood there, watching.

The gray van's side cargo door was opening.

The green van made a sharp left, churning browned winter grass in the wake of its rear tires. It reached the sidewalk, knocking over a wooden-and-wrought-iron bench, bouncing the curb and crossing the street, then bouncing the curb again, on the grass, coming up the midway. The gray van was almost even with it on one side, the blue sedan with the damaged fender coming up on its other flank. A moon roof opened in the blue sedan and a man pushed through the hole.

Holden started moving away from the rostrum, moving forward along the stage erected for the ceremonies, the board creaking under his feet as he increased his pace. "Liz! Liz! Get the kids out of here!"

Holden jumped from the stage, seeing Elizabeth starting to rise from her seat, Irene swept into her arms. Meg stood. Dave was starting to stand, looking around behind him. Two rows farther back Holden saw Rufus

Burroughs standing up, a blur of motion in the strong sun as Burroughs's gun came from the holster.

"Liz!"

The first shots came. From the man in the moon roof of the blue sedan, ear-splittingly loud somehow, a long burst that seemed unending.

The green van's door slid open as it made a half bootlegger and stopped.

Gunfire—heavy-machine-gunfire—came from the open door, screaming from the men and women assembled for the convocation.

Men with automatic weapons were pouring out of the gray van now.

A woman in a blue floral print dress fell dead at Holden's feet, several of the blue flowers with spreading, sticky-looking red centers. Holden nearly tripped over her body.

"Liz!"

He saw Annette Burroughs, sitting in the front row of students, taking the mortarboard from her head as she stood up, a look of confusion in her eyes.

Ski-masked men with automatic weapons were running up the center aisle along the grass, firing right and left. Holden threw himself toward the nearest of them, under the muzzle of the gun, the gun crashing down across his back as his hands grabbed at the man's legs behind the knees. Holden threw him down, the M16 firing out skyward. Holden reached for the rifle, knowing it was empty, grabbing for it anyway. Another ski-masked man's rifle jammed. Holden inverted the M16 in his hands, the flesh of the palms burning as skin contacted bare metal. He swung the M16, the buttstock breaking as it contacted the other weapon. But he swatted it away.

Holden heard a scream. He saw Annette Burroughs. One of the ski-masked men was bringing the muzzle of his rifle on line toward her. Holden threw himself onto her, bulldogging her to the ground and away from the gun. Holden looked up, the assault rifle swinging down on him. He started to jump for the man, knowing he'd never make it. There was a loud boom, then another and another, the ski-masked man's body twisting around, a gunshot wound spraying blood from the left side of his neck, his M16 spraying death into the crowd as he fell, Annette Burroughs screaming, Holden's left hand suddenly alive with pain, then just as suddenly numbed, a starburst filling his eyes as he fell back.

Holden looked at Annette Burroughs. She was dead, shot at least a half-dozen times.

Holden was up, the heavy roar of the machine gun from the open door of the van unceasing.

He was moving. He saw Elizabeth, her little revolver firing point blank from her right hand, Irene clutched against her in her left arm. Her attacker fell. Elizabeth turned toward the hedgerow to the right of the speakers' platform. Another of the ski-masked gunmen came at her. Elizabeth spun toward him. "Liz!"

"David!"

She fired, the man with the ski mask firing, her body starting to twist away from the bullets. "Liz!" The revolver fell from her hand. Holden was shoving people aside, tripping over people cowering on the ground between the seats. "Liz!" Holden fell, pushed up—he saw her, both his wife's arms cocooning Irene. Meg reached out for them, tried shielding them with her own body, her light-colored dress showing the splotches of blood, the tearing furrows as they plowed across her back. Liz and Meg, hugging Irene between them, began to fall, the gunman still firing.

Holden lurched over a dead woman and a child, fighting his way toward them.

He saw Dave. Dave threw himself on the man who had just—killed? Dave threw himself on the man, Dave's hand closing over the man's face, Dave's right fist hammering at the face. The man went down. Dave stood there, turned toward his mother and sisters, their bodies caught up in the hedgerow, arms still intertwined. The machine gun—it had been silent for an instant. It started again. Holden ran, throwing himself toward his son. "Dave! Get down! My God! Dave!" The machine gun's path intersected Dave's body, Dave slammed into the hedgerow, leaves and branches spraying up everywhere, Dave's body twitching, twisting, his eyes wide. Holden's throat ached with screaming.

"Dave!"

There was a blur of motion at his left and he started to turn toward it, heard the burst of gunfire, felt the shattering pain and sudden nausea, his eyes sharp-focused as he spilled forward. He thought he saw Rufus Burroughs getting killed, but he wasn't sure. Holden tried to get his legs going.

"Li-i-i-z!"

It was a wave, of red, black, and everything and nothing and it crashed over his face and drowned him.

CHAPTER
15

David Holden heard crying.

"Irene?" He looked toward the sound. There was a woman lying beside him. But she wasn't Elizabeth. He could tell from the color of her hair—blond—above the bandages that masked her face—masks. He closed his eyes and pain washed over him. Masks. The green van. The gray van. The blue sedan. The men with ski masks covering their faces. The automatic weapons.

"Liz!" He screamed the name and tried to sit up and he saw a blur of red-stained white and felt hands pressing against his shoulders as the pain flooded over him again. Again? The pain was everywhere. . . . Holden opened his eyes. He turned his head left. Where the woman with blond hair had been there was a human-shaped mound covered with a gray blanket that had *US* stenciled on it in black. He saw two men. He squinted his eyes tight shut for an instant. . . . He opened them. The mound was gone. He closed his eyes. . . . "Take it easy, fella. Gotta move ya a little." Holden looked up into a face. A boy in his late teens, a green baseball cap masking half his face in shadow. . . . "Liz?" . . . . "All right, sir, can you drink this?" Her hair wasn't as dark as Elizabeth's and she had brown eyes. She was dressed oddly, a green jacket over a white dress. He felt water on his lips, started to choke, and the pain flooded over him again. . . . "Doctor Holden? Try some of this." It was the woman's voice again and he opened his eyes. She wasn't wearing the jacket anymore and she looked very tired. There was sunlight. A lot of it, and it hurt his eyes. "This is broth. You need your strength. I have some Jell-O for you. How about that?" He started to speak to her and he heard somebody's voice, "Stat! Stat!" The woman was gone. . . . "Liz? Irene? Meg? Dave? Dave?" He was cold. "I'm cold!" His body shook. "Easy, man," a voice told him, and he felt the scratchiness of wool under his chin and his body trembled more and his eyes weren't open anymore. . . . "Doctor Holden?"

David Holden looked up. It was the nurse he had seen before. She was wearing the green jacket again. "My wife. My children."

"I don't have all the casualty reports. There have been so many. We had to set up these tents on the commons for the less seriously wounded or the ones who couldn't be moved at all."

"My family?"

"A pretty, dark-haired woman and a girl in her early teens who looked just like her?"

"They would have had a little girl with my coloring."

The nurse's eyes flooded with tears. "I'm sorry." She shook her head. "They were holding the little girl. None of them—I'm sorry."

Holden felt the tears welling up in his eyes. "My son?"

"What'd—I don't—"

"Big for his age. Twelve. Real tall and well built and just the finest looking—"

"Him, too, I think. Was—was he wearing a blue jacket and gray slacks?"

Holden heard the sounds of his own sobbing, as though the sound were from somebody else, his throat so tight he couldn't breathe properly, and it was hard to swallow the saliva. His nose was running. His eyes hurt. His fists hammered against his thighs.

"Don't do that! Your arm."

"My . . ." He couldn't speak, the pressure in his head killing him, his body shaking.

"Doctor Stephenson! Doctor Stephenson! Hurry!"

His temples throbbed. His breath—he was choking. . . .

"Doctor Holden."

He opened his eyes. A man in a business suit and sunglasses.

"Doctor Holden. Can you hear me?"

It was a black suit. Maybe he was a mortician? But why sunglasses?

"Doctor Holden. Blink if you understand me. Okay?"

Holden, his voice not sounding like his own voice, said, "Who are you?"

"All right. I'm Hal Robinson. I'm a special agent with the FBI."

"Was that a dream—a nightmare—I mean—my wife and children—"

The man—he was black—consulted a notebook. The

notebook was black like his suit. "Elizabeth Margaret Holden, Margaret Louise Holden, David Richard Holden, Jr., Irene Marian Holden. Yes, sir."

The tears came again, the tightness in his throat again.

"I have to ask you some questions, Doctor Holden."

"Annette Burroughs?"

"Lemme see." He flipped through the notebook again. "Yes, sir. Now—will you answer some questions for me, sir?"

"Dean Putnam? Rufus Burroughs? Humphrey Hodges?"

"I can't go through the entire damn list, Doctor Holden. There were forty-three people killed here. Another ninety-two were seriously injured and a couple dozen more had minor injuries and were immediately released."

"Answer me, damn you!" It still wasn't his voice talking, but it would do until his own voice came back. He couldn't see beyond a blur now, the tears filling his eyes and his hands and arms too tired to move up and brush them away. And they would only come back. His head hurt and his left side—there was something wrong with his left side.

"Putnam's around here, so he can't be too seriously wounded. We got all the really bad ones out by last night."

"Last night?"

"It was three days ago, Doctor Holden. All right—this Burroughs guy. A cop?"

Holden nodded.

"Released from here. Apparently wasn't anything serious. And what was the other name?"

"Two more. Doctor Sheila Lord. Doctor Humphrey Hodges."

"Doctor Sheila Lord—okay. I'm sorry." Holden closed his eyes. "Humphrey Martin Hodges? He isn't on my list. Mustn't have been injured. This is pretty accurate."

David Holden started to laugh.

"Look, Doctor Holden. These questions, huh?"

His eyes still weren't clear. He nodded and his head, his whole body, ached.

"Okay. When we found Mrs. Holden, she had a gun in her hand. It was a Smith & Wesson Chiefs Special, thirty-eight Special caliber blue. We ran the gun and found out it was yellow-formed out to you from—let's see—a man named Hobson, doing business as Hobson's—"

"So what?"

"Mrs. Holden had no permit to carry a concealed weapon, Doctor. Why was she carrying a gun? Did you have any prior knowledge of this attack? Otherwise, why was she—"

"Did you catch all the people who did this?"

"No, sir. But the investigation is moving ahead."

"Why did you waste time investigating a dead woman who died with two of her children in her arms?"

"Normal people don't run around packing a gun, Doctor."

"Maybe they should have."

"Why was she carrying the gun, Doctor Holden? We're talking about a violation of statutes concerning concealed weapons carry and possible charges against you for aiding and abetting. Now, nobody's looking to give you a hard time. But I can have the local boys over here to push it if you don't answer my question, Doctor. Why was she carrying a gun?"

"Because I loved her. I wanted her to stay alive."

"But that still doesn't answer—"

"Then fuck off and die," Holden told him, closing his eyes.

CHAPTER
16

His clothes smelled of bandages and body odor and the field shower he'd taken hadn't helped at all, too much of his body covered with bandages to get really clean. His left shoulder, his left rib cage, his left thigh. They had taken three 5.56mm bullets out of him, and after he'd gone unconscious, a grenade had apparently exploded near enough to him that he'd picked up a small piece of shrapnel in his right forearm. His left hand was the most heavily bandaged, the most seriously wounded part.

They had told him to consult with his family physician. He had asked for his wife's gun back. It was being impounded as evidence and he could write to the proper authorities. He was even given the proper address. Holden gave no proper thank you.

The Ford station wagon was where he'd parked it, the right front fender heavily dinged—he didn't know by what—but the vehicle otherwise untouched. He didn't open the rear deck until he was several miles away from

Thomas Jefferson University and certain he wasn't being followed or otherwise watched. But his Levi's and boots and the shirt and socks he'd worn to go shooting with Rufus Burroughs were still on top of the tarp.

Underneath the tarp he had brought along for use when firing the rifle prone, the carpet seemed undisturbed. He rolled back the tarp and the carpet and used the fatter of the two keys to open the rear seat compartment, the fold-down seats closing together to form a trunk of sorts. His H & K 91 rifle was still in the plastic case he'd gotten for it, packed in at a bizarre angle in the confined space, but untouched. The two Berettas were there, the Crain knife, all of his gear. He reclosed the folding seats and relocked them. He had already checked the glove compartment. The .45 he habitually carried there was still in place.

Holden drove on, forcing thought out of his mind. With thought came grief.

He turned on the radio to the all-news station. The terrorist acts of three days ago and since were the news. By Executive Order, a temporary ban was in effect on the sale of all firearms, ammunition, and explosives, the sale of gasoline except directly into the tank or approved containers in quantities of a gallon or less, the sale of alcohol other than beer or wine. Any firearms found outside the home or business of the person legally owning them would be confiscated until the state of emergency prompting the regulations had passed.

The day of the convocation saw one hundred eighteen terrorist bombings, attacks (such as that at Thomas Jefferson University, one of nineteen colleges or universities so affected) and major but unspecified acts of sabotage.

Holden wondered almost absently how high the real number had to have been to let out an official number such as one hundred eighteen? Limited martial law had been declared in specific geographic areas, and, in most municipalities around the country, police had been given shoot-to-kill orders when confronting persons for whom just cause existed to believe they were engaged in terrorist acts.

And there was a name, although the government officially denied having known of the existence of such a group prior to the events of three days ago. A name of a group claiming responsibility for the events, claiming also that this was just the beginning. The name was the Front for the Liberation of North America. The FLNA had released a manifesto to all the major networks and newspapers, not only assuming responsibility and threatening more acts against "the fascist dictatorship of the so-called United States" but claiming to do so in the cause of freedom for persecuted minorities within the country, to include all the traditional minorities and youth as well. Until "the corrupt, monied industrialist power brokers" announced their intention "to dissolve traditional government and lay power in the hands of a revolutionary provisional government pending free elections" there would be bloodshed, the responsibility for the violence laid at the feet of the government.

Holden shut off the radio as he turned into the driveway. The house was secluded enough, but it would be best to remove the weapons from the car when it was parked in the garage, out of sight.

If the telephone worked, he had to call Elizabeth's parents, tell them.

Funeral arrangements. He had buried his father and mother. He knew how that went.

Holden took the .45 from the glove compartment and put it into the waistband of his trousers under his jacket.

He got out and locked the car.

He stared at the front porch.

He didn't know how long he stood there. His watch had been smashed anyway during, during what had happened. He had never bought a good watch again after selling the Rolex he'd worn in the SEALs, but the money it had brought had paid for books. Otherwise, it would have been harder than it had already been to put food on the table.

At last, Holden realized he was walking up the steps, turning the key in the lock.

He walked inside.

Did he close the door behind him? He didn't remember.

Was there electricity? He didn't turn on the lights.

He looked into the recreation room. No one watched the television, no one listened to the stereo. The VCR's clock blinked "12:00" over and over. There had been a blackout. Was the food in the freezer ruined? He walked into the kitchen but didn't bother to look. He leaned against the kitchen counter. He stared at the refrigerator. The pink-and-red construction-paper heart Irene had made—*I Love You Mommie + Daddy* —was still magneted to the door.

The tightness was coming in his throat again.

He started from the kitchen, and just inside the back door on the other side of the counter, he saw Dave's skateboard on the floor. He went over to it, picked it up, carefully, something he had never done, read the slogans and catchphrases stickered all over the underside, each sticker representing some of Dave's money spent customizing it. He rolled the wheels with his thumbs as he set it down on the counter upside down. Were the "trucks" that supported the wheels tight enough but not too tight?

Holden realized he was biting his lower lip.

He left the kitchen, his left hand hurting him, the pain medicine wearing off now. He stopped as he approached the stairs. He looked at the telephone, closed his eyes—*Well, so I told her I wouldn't get my hair cut like that. It was just awful? I mean, tack-ee?*—"Meg," Holden whispered.

He leaned heavily on the banister, started up the stairs. At the height of the stairs, he turned, looked down. The door was still open.

And what did that matter?

He walked into the hallway, looking down its length at the childrens' rooms. But he turned into the room he had shared with Elizabeth ever since they had scraped together enough for a down payment and convinced a bank to trust them with a fixed-rate mortgage.

Holden stood in the doorway.

The double bed was made.

He walked toward it, rolled back the bedspread, Elizabeth's nightgown on the pillow where she always left it. It was white, ankle length. He had bought it for her.

Holden took the .45 from his waistband and winced with the pain as he used his left hand to work back the slide. He let it skate forward, chamber loaded now, the hammer cocked. His right thumb pushed up the safety. He let the pistol fall from his hand onto the bed, the mattress sagging for an instant to absorb the kinetic energy of the decelerating falling body.

Who cared?

"Liz . . ."

Holden sat on the edge of the bed, picking up the nightgown. He held it to his face. Its fabric carried her scent still, and the scent of her perfume, of her hair.

Holden slid off the edge of the bed as he sagged forward, still holding her nightgown in his right hand, tears flooding his eyes, the bedspread sliding partially off the bed as well. As Holden knelt there, through his tears he could see the .45.

His fingers opened and the nightgown slipped through them. His fingers closed over the butt of the pistol.

"I can't . . ."

There was no use, no use to anything.

Holden's thumb eased down the safety.

There was the grip safety to consider, of course. He turned the pistol around in his hand, his body aching all over and the tightness of his throat worse than it had ever been. His right thumb slid through the trigger guard, his fingers trying to close tightly enough on the grip to keep the safety depressed. But he had no strength. He shifted the gun once again in his grasp. If he cocked his wrist, he could do it all right.

His fist closed around the butt, the grip safety fully depressed.

Holden brought the muzzle of the gun to his mouth, opened his mouth, tasted the copperiness of it. He rested his face forward, against his wife's nightgown. He couldn't smell the smells of her so strongly now; the taste of the metal obscured them.

He wanted to speak.

He wanted to say her name.

He closed his eyes.

There was nothing left.

He felt the softness of the fabric against his face.

His right first finger entered the trigger guard.

His eyes brimmed tears.

He wanted to say her name one more time.

Holden eased the muzzle of the pistol from his mouth.

He looked at the nightgown.

"Liz."

He started the muzzle to his mouth, his eyes closing. He had the smell of her again and must do it quickly before he lost it again.

"She wouldn't want ya to, man. Put it down."

Holden kept his eyes closed. His lips brushed at the muzzle of the pistol as he spoke. "Go away, Burroughs." He could smell the oil on the gun. It was too late.

"You're damn right. I'm not gonna watch ya make an asshole outta yourself. What the hell ya think she'd say?"

"She can't say anything."

"You just gonna let the motherfuckers get away with it and blow your damn brains out?"

"Yeah."

"Hell—don't let me stop ya."

Holden held the gun by his lips.

His right thumb touched at the safety. He raised it, dropped the gun on the bed again, and as he turned around there on his knees, the nightgown caught on his clothes and fell across his right leg. Holden looked down at it.

"Change your mind?"

Holden shrugged his shoulders, his eyes not focused on anything but her nightgown.

"You can make a difference, man! Why the hell you think I didn't do what you were gonna do?"

"Maybe it comes in multiples. You lost one wife. I lost one wife and three children."

"Annette's parents—they never even got outta high school, man! High school! And there she was, gettin' her master's degree just like some white woman—God damn it!"

"Lots of white women don't have master's degrees, Rufus."

"You know—God damn it, you know!"

"You wanna borrow the gun?" Holden looked up from his knees at Burroughs's face, noticing for the first time the bandage over his left eyebrow and the general discolorization of the left side of his dark-brown face. "Or did you bring your own?"

"I'm not dyin'! Those murderin' motherfuckers are history! You should know all about history, Holden! I'm findin' 'em, I'm gonna rip their damn heads off."

"Shooting 'em's neater. You want a drink?"

"Yeah."

"How'd you get in?"

"The car was in the driveway, the door was open. Nobody was downstairs. I figured you might be . . . I drove by the university. I just missed ya."

Holden stood up and Elizabeth's gown fell from his leg to the floor. He bent over, picked it up.

"She was a real lady, man—ya know?"

"I know. So was yours."

"Yeah."

Gently, Holden placed the nightgown on her pillow, then drew the bedspread up over it.

She was gone, but she would never be gone.

Holden looked at Burroughs. "You stopped me from killing myself. I'll let you know later if it was a good idea. Let's have the drink."

"All right."

Holden only nodded, hearing Elizabeth's voice in his head saying, "Okay, David."

CHAPTER

17

The television newscaster was telling everybody that there had been unexplained fires and explosions in several major cities, but informed sources indicated the incidents had nothing to do with the terrorist attacks by the Front for the Liberation of North America.

"Shoot the fuckin' television, Rufe."

"Hey—no, man."

"Fine."

"There's a news blackout, they told us."

Holden looked at Rufus Burroughs. "There's not only a blackout," he began, stabbing his index finger toward Burroughs, "but a whiteout, too," and he stabbed his thumb at himself.

"You don't drink all the time."

"Only sometimes. But it's not like it'll get to be a habit. You can't buy the stuff anymore."

"I know."

Holden drained his glass, set it on the coffee table,

and slumped back into the couch. His wounds were hurting him. "You're not going to make it, Rufe."

"Why?"

"They'll find out about you. Not this damn Front for the Liberation of North America crowd, but the Feds. They'll pull your plug."

"Rosie Shepherd knows where I can find this Leopards gang. It was kids that killed my partner, Clyde Ramirez. Those were the last words he said. It was kids that killed Annette. And your wife and kids, man."

"You'll never pull it off. The Feds are more concerned with people fighting back than getting the bastards behind this. Self-defense is no longer socially acceptable. Did I tell you about that crap about my wife's gun?" He felt the tightness in his throat. He didn't want more whiskey.

"I'm more concerned about getting the people who did this than anything, David. Anything I've ever been concerned about in my life. More than anything. And so are the men and the women helpin' me. You can do it, too, man."

"Hey—more power to you, okay? But your chances of making it are about as good as your chances of flying without a damn airplane, Rufe."

"Then what the fuck am I supposed to do, David? I mean, I'm black, right? And these assholes are sayin' they're representin' me? You know what that's gonna cause for every minority group in this country? Heaps of shit. What the hell am I supposed to do?"

Holden considered the request for illumination. After some seconds he answered, "Damned if I know. See, it's not that I know what to do, but I know what not to do. See?"

"No."

"All you're going to do is bring the law down all over you like a cheap tent."

"Then that's the way it'll happen."

"What good are you going to do when you're dead or in jail, Rufe? Huh? When I was going to splash my brains all over the ceiling up there, you were telling me my wife and the kids wouldn't have wanted me to do it. You were right, okay? But your wife wouldn't have wanted you to violate the law you're sworn to uphold. I'm not going to kill myself—at least not today. You throw away the law, you're doing the same thing, though. Just killing yourself in a different way. These clowns want guys like you to take up a gun and go after them. They want as much violence as they can generate."

"Can't say I'm not obligin', then, can they?"

"My head hurts. My whole body hurts. But my insides hurt more, man." Holden leaned forward, took a cigarette from the box, and lit it. He shoved the box over toward Rufus Burroughs. Burroughs lit up. "If I thought going out hunting these bastards would bring my family back, or even avenge them, hell. You wouldn't have to ask twice, Rufe. All it's going to do is make things worse. The government may be damn slow, but the FBI'll nail them. And that's the way it's supposed to be. By you staying on as a cop and working inside the law, you can do more. It may not give instant gratification, but putting these crazies on trial and revealing whoever is behind them is the way, man. It's the only way."

"David, you're a good man, but you're full of shit. I got funeral arrangements to make—ahh . . ." Burroughs head slumped forward and he began to cry, heavy sobs, his body racked with them. David Holden— his left side screamed at him when he moved—managed to get his arm around his friend's shoulders.

CHAPTER
18

There were so many funerals, there wasn't the opportunity to select a date. The funeral of Annette Burroughs and the funerals of Holden's wife and children were on the same day, almost at the same hour, but on opposite sides of the county. There was a shortage of coffins, so Holden had taken what he could, the color of the lining and the pillow beneath Elizabeth's head a kind of sick shade of lavender which she had never liked in life. There had been no child's coffin of proper size for Irene, so it had been a matter of waiting until deliveries caught up and burying her separately or burying her in an adult coffin like her mother, sister, and brother. He had decided on an adult coffin.

All the things that made people want to die had been necessary—selection of the vault into which the coffin would be placed, selection of a favorite hymn, selection of what to do in lieu of flowers. The mortuary people had been kind about the money. He would pay when the check came for his book cover. That plus the money he could scrape out of his next paycheck—Thomas Jefferson University would reopen soon with a limited class schedule—would take care of most of it if he let himself be late on some other bills.

The cemetery people had wanted the grave opening and closing fees up front. He'd found the money. The lots had been left to him by his own mother and father.

He'd gone to the airport, armed security police checking cars as they entered the access ramps, the delays impossibly long. But Holden had heard about the security checks and left his .45 at home, hidden with the rest of his guns and gear.

Eventually, he'd reached the terminal, a physical search and a wanding necessary to enter, then the usual electronic security—only it seemed to take longer—when he had gone to the gate. Thomas and Diane Ashbrooke, Thomas in a dark-blue suit, Diane in a dark-gray suit, had come through the walkway and stopped, staring at him. They both looked exactly as he remembered them from a year ago Christmas. This past Christmas, they had been in Europe. Tom was tall, very fit looking for a man somewhere in his mid-sixties; and, Diane, of course, was beautiful. Perfect steel-gray hair, perfectly styled, perfect figure, perfect clothes, perfect makeup. She was fifty-four exactly, only a teenager when Elizabeth was born to her.

Hesitantly, Holden walked toward them. Diane Ashbrooke ran to him and put her arms around his neck. Even her perfume smelled somehow "perfect." "Ohh, David—my God."

He held her because she wanted him to, he knew. Thomas Ashbrooke stood behind her and extended his hand. "David."

"Tom."

"I wish—I don't know what I wish. You're living."

"Yeah."

"I know. I really do, David."

David Holden doubted his father-in-law knew at all. . . .

He resented Diane touching anything in Elizabeth's kitchen. But he sat at the kitchen table, Tom Ashbrooke across from him, listening to the sounds of Diane making dinner, and said nothing about it.

"David. I'm going to lay my cards on the table. There are other things we need to talk about, but you're going to need some help. And we can help. We want to help. We never got along terrifically, but in our own way, Diane and I always looked on you like a son. And now, more than ever, we want to help."

"Thanks. I'll do all right."

"No—listen. For openers, let us help with the funeral expenses. Money hasn't been in short supply for me since I can't remember when."

Holden looked into his father-in-law's blue eyes, exactly like Elizabeth's eyes only there was a hardness there she'd never had. "Liz and I never took money from you guys when she was alive. I'm not doing it now. I mean, thanks. I really mean that. I appreciate the sentiment behind the offer. But I'm handling it."

Tom looked into his spatulate-fingered hands.

Diane spoke. Holden didn't turn around to look at her. Over her dress she was wearing the apron Irene had worn when she'd helped Elizabeth in the kitchen. "Tom and I miss Liz and the children just as much as you do, David. And I know it hurts to hear that. We miss them in ways you can't understand. You miss them in ways we could never understand. But neither of us wants this to be the last time we see you, as if our whole family died because four of us are gone. The three of us are a family now, David."

Tom Ashbrooke spoke, his voice low. "She's right. I know you never gave two shits for us. Fine. I didn't hit it off with Diane's parents because of the difference in our ages. But we can take this as an opportunity. Liz would want that, David. She loved you and she loved us. She wouldn't want it to end this way."

"Tom is right, David. He really is!"

Holden didn't say anything. . . .

Diane had been a nurse and he had done what she insisted upon before dressing for the funeral: take a full shower and damn the bandages. She had rebandaged the wounds for him, telling him they were largely superficial except for the left hand and the shrapnel wound. He'd put a plastic bag over his hand and tried to keep the shrapnel wound out of the water as much as possible anyway.

They had driven to the funeral home. There had been no wake. Their minister was there, looking very tired. There had been many funerals and were many more still to come. Humphrey Hodges was there. Dean Putnam was there. Some of the kids from the school Meg and Dave had attended and the corresponding parents saying, "How terrible!" and "How dreadful" and one man even saying, "I hope they get the fuckers that did it," but none of the parents really knowing Meg and Dave as anything more than two kids their own kids "hung around" with.

Some neighbors. Some friends. Irene's Sunday-school teacher, her children (Irene's age) left with relatives.

Holden sat staring out the limousine window, Diane, sitting between him and Tom, holding his right hand tightly. He kept his eyes turned toward the dark tinted glass.

At the cemetery there were two other funerals in progress and it was necessary to wait for fifteen minutes before beginning the funeral because the machine used for opening the graves had broken down but was all right now. "God—we're getting so behind," the man in the gray suit and accommodating plastic smile said, by way of excuse. If he'd said, "We're buried in work," or something like that, Holden had thought, he would have strangled the man with his bare hands.

Holden stood beside the holes in the ground at the center of the four graves.

The minister talked about ashes and dust and lost youth and eternal life and the mysteries of God's will and carrying on and what a wonderful woman Elizabeth had been and what fine Christian children Meg and Dave and Irene had been.

The coffins were all the same color and Holden was suddenly unsure if they had gotten it right and had the right body going into the right grave.

He tried very hard to hold it in, but fell on his knees weeping.

Holden stayed beside the graves until they were closed.

He didn't want the cemetery people rushing the machinery away and leaving them uncovered.

He stayed by the graves after they were closed, all the others who had come gone, hearing Tom telling the limousine driver, "Then go to hell if you don't want to wait!"

"David?"

"What, Diane?"

"It's time to go, now."

"I know."

"Then, come with me."

David Holden didn't want to go with anyone except the four he would be leaving behind. He had tried going with them.

CHAPTER
19

Rose Shepherd stepped up into the van, slipping off
her lined rain parka. Rufus Burroughs called after her as
he started to slide the door closed, "Two minutes, Rosie."

"Right." As the door slammed, she was already opening the button at the waistband of her skirt. She could
hear Rufus and the other two men talking outside. Kicking her shoes off, she started pushing her skirt down
over her hips. If she had gotten her information wrong
—but she put the thought out of her mind.

She pushed her slip off, catching up both garments
and throwing them over the back of the swiveling passenger seat nearest her. Was this the right thing, to take
the law into one's own hands? Rose Shepherd wondered. She sat down on the other chair, opening the
black canvas bag and taking out the black boot socks,
pulling them on over her nylons, no time to take her
panties off and then the panty hose. "Damn!" One of

her nails caught at the toe of her left foot, but she didn't think she'd started a run.

She took the black battle-dress utility pants from her bag as well, stuffing both feet into them before she stood up, hitching them up to her waist. Her hands undid the bow at the collar of her gray blouse, then worked open the buttons down the front and at the cuffs. She shrugged out of it, quickly checking the Smith & Wesson Model 60 .38 Special in the Null SKR upside-down shoulder holster. The holster body was white, translucent high density polymer, heat molded and sixty thousandths of an inch thick. The harness—thin white synthetic as well—suspended the revolver just beneath and slightly forward of her left armpit, crossed over her shoulders, and, rather than securing it to the belt as a man might do when worn over a shirt, she had shortened the crossover strap so it secured to her bra. Under a "blousy" blouse, it didn't show at all, but to get to what she considered her last-ditch, hideout gun, all that was necessary was to open a single button and reach beneath the blouse. She skinned into a black T-shirt, the gun showing easily now because of the tightness, but she was among friends. "I'm decent—go for it!" she called out, rising up on her toes and tugging at the zipper of her BDU pants.

The farmhouse was painted white and set well back behind high poplar trees, which hadn't grown here naturally. From the little-traveled, dirt ranch road, the house was barely visible at all, even with the leaves gone from the trees, and from up close, because of the way the pine trees were rowed, it was impossible to see beyond the house into the several heavily wooded acres immediately behind, the woods there being pines as well. The farm was a mile or better from the nearest two-lane highway, and, as Rosie Shepherd had told them, the farms on both sides had been bought up but no one lived on them. It was as secluded as one could get around here, yet still within striking distance of civilization.

Rufus Burroughs eyed the white horizontal slat fence, saw the wires running along it. There were no signs of microphones, so he assumed the wires were some sort of electronic warning system or electrification. Rosie Shepherd, her brown hair covered by a black, silk-looking bandana, the bandana identical to the one that covered the lower half of her face beneath the dark camouflage-stick makeup, met his eyes, her green eyes flickering back to the fence.

There were a few cows in the pasture, their udders bloated, looking as if they hadn't been milked yet and were overdue for it. He'd spent half his youth on a farm.

"Can't be any pressure-sensitive stuff," Rosie whispered, the bandana puffing in and out over her mouth as she spoke, "or else the animals would set it off all the time."

"I'll boost you over the fence. Check it out," Burroughs told her. He looked to left and right, saw nothing (although they could have been observed from the farmhouse through binoculars or monitored by parabolic microphone), and told her, "Let's do it."

She came to him quickly and he swept her up into his arms. For a moment his mind filled with thoughts of his dead wife, the last time he had held a woman so close. Burroughs raised her high over the level of the fence,

trying to avoid touching it, Rosie jumped from his arms
to the ground on the other side as nimbly as a child.

He reached down to the ground beside him, grabbed
her H & K 94 9mm carbine and passed it over the fence
quickly, then she was off at a dead run. He ducked back
into the ditch and checked his wristwatch, giving her
ten minutes mentally before he'd consider her overdue,
fifteen minutes before he'd go after her. . . .

She huddled down in the depression, the ground beneath the trees here littered with pine needles. Her
knees were almost up to her chin, the H & K 94 tight
against her chest in both fists. There was a swarm of
black flies near her face, despite the season, and she was
glad for the scarf covering her hair. She blew at the flies
to get them away from her.

There were nine men, one of them older-looking, the
others recognizable as Leopards. The older man
seemed in his late thirties or early forties. She had seen
him somewhere. On the street with the Leopards?
There was some kind of field equipment stacked neatly
on the ground a few yards beyond where they stood,
backpacks or satchels, M16's or illegally converted
AR-15 rifles leaned casually here and there among the
gear.

And Rose Shepherd recognized what the nine men
were doing. Her father had been a police officer. Her
ambition, ever since she was a little girl and had realized that there were women police officers, too, had
been to be a cop just like her dad. In high school, while
the other girls had been at cheerleading practice, she
had studied martial arts. What she was watching was a
drill in unarmed defense against an opponent armed
with a knife. The one who had done the last two sets—it

was Reefer—was very good at it, or else his opponents were unimaginably clumsy. Maybe it was a combination of both. Or was this older man just a very good teacher?

She had seen an innocuous-enough looking man in well-worn bib overalls and straw cowboy hat heading out toward the pasture that paralleled the road, presumably to bring the cows in and relieve them. Her breasts ached when her period was overdue—which it was now—and she could sympathize in a way. But why hadn't the cows been milked yet? She had never been a farm girl, but in movies at least she had always thought they were milked during the predawn hours.

More men were coming out of the farmhouse, five of them, each of the men fit-looking regardless of height, some tall enough, one of them shorter than her own five foot seven. Each was armed with a pistol carried in plain view, four in shoulder holsters, one in a military-style flap holster similar to the one at her right hip.

They joined the adult male subject already there with the Leopards.

There was another quick fall, neither of these two Leopards as good as Reefer had revealed himself to be.

And then she saw Smitty coming out of the house. Smitty, the leader of the Leopards, wore a shoulder holster over his black T-shirt and there was a knife sheathed at his belt. Rather than joining the rest of his gang, he fell into the knot of five men already surrounding the first man. Did he hold some leadership function here, as well?

The first man began to address everyone there. She could hear that he was speaking, but not distinguish any of his words at the distance, some two hundred yards.

Rose Shepherd looked at her wristwatch, a plain lady's Rolex that her parents had given her when she'd graduated from college and been accepted at the police academy. She had been over the fence on recon for ten minutes. Soon, Rufus Burroughs would come looking for her and that would blow the whole thing. As quietly as she could, she started edging back on knees and elbows, at least fifty yards to cover before she'd feel safe getting up into a crouch and running. . . .

Rufus Burroughs checked the Seiko on his wrist. Fifteen minutes. If something had happened to Rosie . . . He started moving back from the fence, just as he heard the engine sounds. He threw himself down into the ditch again, trying to make out the direction from which they came. From the picturesquely painted white-trimmed red barn a hundred yards or so to the west of the house. It sounded like a missing head pipe or cracked manifold and suddenly something clicked in his mind: One of the much censored police reports he had read of the incident at Thomas Jefferson University had included a remark by one of the survivors, a woman, if he remembered it right. She'd said that the blue sedan with the dented fender and the moon roof had sounded as if it needed a muffler.

Burroughs pushed himself up, edging back toward the fence on knees and elbows. He raised his binoculars and focused toward the barn.

Burroughs swallowed hard. Two vans, one gray and one green, and a blue sedan with a crushed front fender. He couldn't swallow at all now, the rage filling him.

These were the ones who had killed his wife.

As he brought down the binoculars—his hands were trembling and his breath was short—he saw Rosie Shepherd, running from tree cover.

He got up into a crouch, signaling her to look behind her toward the barn. She kept coming, her carbine at high port.

Burroughs started for the fence.

As Rosie neared it, she tossed him the carbine. He caught it. "The Leopards. Five other guys in military gear. A guy in a sport jacket. I saw the last guy on the street with Smitty or Reefer—I can't remember."

"Get yourself over the fence, girl. They're comin' out to party and those are the vehicles used in the attack on the university."

"Shit," she hissed.

Rosie Shepherd looked around left and right. "There's no way over the fence without hitting the wires. What's the plan?"

"We follow 'em, pull their plug before they do their thing."

"Too many of them, Rufe. I saw automatic weapons."

"Tough. Here—" He tossed the carbine back over the fence to her and she caught it. "We'll pick you up—stay down."

She started running back into the trees, Burroughs backing away toward the ditch, his fists balling on the AR-15. "Time to kick ass and take names," Rufus Burroughs hissed. . . .

Rosie Shepherd hid just inside the tree line, working the H & K 94's bolt and chambering a round, leaving the safety off, ready. If it had been an MP 5 submachine gun like they had in the Metro Central arsenal, she would have felt more comfortable. But once the attacks had begun, a departmental directive had come down that no automatic weapons were to be signed out without two authorizations, one from downtown, including privately owned automatic weapons that some officers kept stored in their precinct gun rooms for emergency use.

It was okay for these terrorists or revolutionaries or whatever they were to have automatic weapons, but bad policy for the police to be similarly equipped so they could fight back.

If her dad were alive, he would have been up on charges or suspended for calling somebody an asshole, she thought, smiling at the memory of him.

The college professor Rufus Burroughs had introduced her to—David Haldeman or Homan or something—had reminded her of her dad, the height, the high forehead, the full shock of dark hair, the humor in his brown eyes. Until his death—he had gone out to pick up a gallon of milk and the "stop and rob" was being hit —he had always looked young, handsome, been vigorous. His death was why she always carried a backup weapon, even off duty, even if it was just a small fighting knife hidden somewhere on her body. There had been three guys at the convenience store and all her father had had on him was a five-shot department-mandated off-duty .38 Special loaded with department-mandated 158-grain round-nosed lead, standard velocity. One of the killers had worn body armor and picked himself up off the floor where her father's bullet had put him and, while her father had been reloading—in those days the department had forbidden the use of speed loaders— the man had shot him five times with a .45.

The two vans and the car were coming up the road, while the man in the bib overalls and cowboy hat walked the cows back toward the barn.

It was ridiculous—vehicles loaded with killers, a farmer taking his cows back for milking.

But, of course, the two vans and the car had been in the barn. Weapons being serviced?

The machine guns that fired from the sides of the vans could have been mounted there, like the door guns on helicopters the guys like Rufus who had been in Vietnam talked about.

She saw Smitty, clearly, sitting in the backseat of the blue sedan, the window rolled down for the pleasant, springlike fresh air and sunshine. Rose Shepherd raised the telescoped H & K's stock, shouldering the weapon, flicking off the safety. She activated the switch for the Aimpoint sight. Even with the target moving, it would be an easy shot.

"Cop," she whispered, resetting the H & K's safety tumbler. She had to let the bad guys shoot first.

She shut off the Aimpoint, leaned back, and memorized license plates. They'd be stolen.

The sedan and then the gray van turned out through the gate. One of the Leopards locked the gate, then hopped back into the van, the dry weather and dirt road combining to cause clouds of dust so great they nearly obscured the vehicles.

As soon as they were over the rise, she ran from cover, toward the fence. No sign of Rufus and the two other guys and their blue van yet. She dropped flat on the ground beside the fence, avoiding a cow patty, but not the smell of it.

The dust cloud had settled. If Rufus had left her behind because of danger—

She heard the screech of the van's brakes, was up— "Damn the fence!"—and flinging a handful of dirt against the fence wires. They weren't electrified. She scrambled over, the van already starting ahead as she jumped inside through the open side door. "I had Smitty right in my sights. I couldn't just assassinate him! Damn!"

"You want them to open up first? You'll get your chance," Rufus told her, then shouted forward, "Step on it, Rudy! Go-go!"

Rufus slammed the door closed.

Rosie Shepherd pulled the bandana down from her face, then the one from her hair, shaking her hair loose, breathing. The air conditioning was on in the van and it felt good. She leaned back in the club chair, the swivel unit locked. "Where do you think they're going, Rufe?"

"Another raid—but this time we stop 'em."

"But where? I mean—"

Rufus Burroughs just shook his head, lit a cigarette and offered her one. She nodded, grateful when he lit it for her; she was too weary to do it herself. Tension, she knew, not exertion—the adrenaline rush, then the crash. Soon, another adrenaline rush. She closed her eyes, inhaling the smoke. . . .

Dimitri Borsoi turned to the one he had told the Leopards to call Abner. Achmed Ferrazzi put down the shortwave handset and headphones. "You were right, Mr. Johnson. Someone was watching us. A few minutes after we left, the intruder detection system on the fence along the roadside was activated. Only once. Probably just one person."

"Give me the headset."

"What's up, Mr. Johnson?"

"We're going to surprise whoever's following us, Smitty. Our car will pull off and so will the other van, while the gray van continues on. Once whoever it is passes our position, we take steps to make certain they can't tell what they know. The scanning monitors at the house haven't picked up any sort of transmission, so whatever they learned is still with them. If we can take one alive, we can get some information. I'd hate to abandon the farm. It's too convenient."

Answering Smitty's seemingly interminable questions was more than annoying, but Smitty was a born man of violence and a born leader to his men. So, worth the bother, for now.

"Johnson to Reefer. Do you read me? Acknowledge."

The radio crackled. "Gotcha, Mr. Johnson."

"Keep monitoring. Jimbo—do you have me too?"

"Sure do, Mr. Johnson."

"Both of you listen, then. Smitty and I have a plan. Reefer. Order your driver to turn off just before the bridge up ahead. We're doing the same. Jimbo, you cross the bridge, go on for about a half a mile, almost up to the highway, then turn around and double back. Whoever is following us will pass your van, Reefer, and the car, then we'll fall in after them. Jimbo, you'll lock them in from ahead. We want a prisoner alive, if possible. All right? This could be the FBI or some small military unit, so be careful. Not just unarmed civilians this time. Understood?"

Reefer and Jimbo tripped over themselves in trying to respond, but he got enough of each transmission to know that they did understand.

And the bridge was just ahead.

CHAPTER

20

David Holden didn't know what to say.

"Will you do me a favor, David? If you won't come with us, at least take this." Tom Ashbrooke, Elizabeth's father—did that still make him his father-in-law? Holden suddenly wondered—extended his right hand and opened his fingers. There was a small key in the palm.

"Please, David?" Diane implored.

"What is it?"

"If you won't come back with us to Switzerland, it's the only thing I can give you that might be of some help. It's the key to a safety deposit box at the main branch of First Liberty. I've made arrangements with the bank's executive vice-president. He owed me a favor. Nothing to sign. Just come in, identify yourself to him—you can trust him—and use the key. If times get really bad here, please."

"I don't—and look, I don't want your money!"

There were so many people moving around them as

the gate area was filling up that it was almost as if the three of them were alone in a room.

"David, dammit! Just take the key. Never use it, then. Just keep it until you need it and if you never need it, fine! All right? There's stubborn and there's stupid. You're pushing into stupid, David. Let us help—if you need it. For Liz's sake, huh?"

"Please, David. Tom and I discussed this. Please?"

David Holden was weary. He took the key. "Fine—satisfied?"

"First Liberty. The fellow's name is Paul Henderson. If something should happen to him, he's left a system in his own papers for you to use the key."

"Fine. Thanks. Look—ahh—I'm just not, ahh—myself, really. I—I appreciate everything you guys, ahh—hell," and he closed his eyes. Diane hugged him, kissed his cheek.

David Holden opened his eyes. Tom Ashbrooke said one word. "Son." And Tom Ashbrooke embraced him. . . .

The van rumbled over the bridge, one of those old wooden affairs that were still seen sometimes out in the country, nothing more than railroad ties and heavy planking to span a stream or where once there had been one. The van slowed.

Rufus Burroughs started to speak. "You get that mask back up on your face, Rosie. Anybody sees we're cops, it's our ass."

"All right, Rufe," but she thought they were already in deeper trouble than they could realize.

"Somethin' wrong, Rufe!" It was Rudy, the driver. "Holy shit! Look behind us!"

Rose Shepherd started out of the club chair, but the van was slipping under her and she was pitched forward, the H & K 94 skating over the shag carpeting that floored the van. She rolled onto her back, more gunfire than she had ever heard at once suddenly all around her, the rear windows blowing inward. She shielded her eyes from the spray of glass. "Rufe!" she screamed.

"Two of 'em—car and a van," Horace Whitelaw shouted. She heard answering fire, rapid semiautomatic bursts from an assault rifle. Rufus Burroughs stood beside the shot-out windows at the rear of the van.

"They suckered us!" Rufus shouted.

She didn't try getting to her feet, but crawled across the van floor on her hands and knees, grabbing up the H & K. It was heavy-machine-gun fire, the walls of the van pinging with it, bullets cutting through the sheet metal, ripping through the club chairs, blowing out the dome light, shattering the side windows outward.

She was beside Rufus Burroughs just as he raised himself up, simultaneously pushing her down. She heard the AR-15 in his hands firing, felt the hot brass pelting at her forehead and left cheek and the left side of her neck.

She was up beside him, swinging the muzzle of the 9mm carbine on line, firing for the windshield of the green van immediately behind them. The roof of the van opened and more machine-gun fire came at them. She ducked, bullets tearing through the rear door panels, chunks of insulation in the air like heavy snowflakes. Something was burning.

Gunfire from the front of the van—but she couldn't see where Horace was hitting. She started to shout to him, but heard Rudy's voice. "Trouble ahead—the gray van—God, they suckered us good! What'll I do, Rufe?"

Rufus started to turn around. "I'll do it!" Rose Shepherd told him, taking off for the front of the van before he could order her otherwise, losing her balance, slamming into the wall of the van, lurching forward. She was on her knees now just between the two front seats of the van. She started to speak.

As she looked up, the gray van was coming dead on for them, men hanging out on both sides, automatic weapons firing. And then the windshield imploded just in front of Rudy and Horace Whitelaw and Rudy screamed, "Mother of God!" And there was nobody driving the van because a chunk of glass the size of a Chinese meat cleaver was through the front of his neck and blood was spraying upward.

Rose Shepherd squinted her eyes against it.

Horace Whitelaw screamed, "My chest—holy—"

Rose Shepherd wasn't even conscious of making a decision. She just started moving. Rudy wasn't big and neither was she. She was beside his dead body in the next instant, her hands on the steering wheel, fighting it, her left foot to the gas pedal because her right foot wouldn't reach around that far. "Hold on!" she shrieked. She had the shot-up van under control now, her eyes crossing over the dashboard, the engine light red for hot. Her left foot stomped the gas pedal to the floor, the van's engine making a hideously loud whine. "Hold on!" And she glared at the gray van, the submachine gunners pulling back inside. "Let's play chicken, motherfucker!"

The gray van was still coming.

She aimed the van right for it, her right hand slipping

from the wheel for an instant to open the flap on the UM-84 holster at her right hip, then back to the wheel.

The gray van swerved just a little and she knew she had him.

She cut the wheel left, the gray van cutting left, to her right, then she cut back right. "Hold on!" She had her foot flat to the floor, her eyes squinting against the impact, her body vibrating with it when it came, the right side mirror torn away, both vans locked together for an instant, the radiator pouring steam in front of her, the sickening burnt smell of antifreeze filling her lungs, the sounds of metal tearing metal, then the gray van gone as her own lurched ahead.

"Rufe! Rufe!"

"Holy—"

"We're not gettin' this van much farther! Rufe! What'll we do, Rufe!?"

"Run her into the ground, Rosie!"

She heard the sound of his assault rifle, the semiautomatic bursts pitiful-sounding to her compared to the automatic-weapons fire of a second or so earlier. The steam was gushing up now, and suddenly it was more than steam, flames licking upward. "Rufus! We're on fire!"

"Keep drivin', Rosie!"

She kept her foot to the floor, the van rocking and jostling around her, the two-lane highway just ahead, stop sign and, just beyond, railroad tracks.

And then she saw it to her right. A train.

"Rufe! Hang on!"

She glanced to the left side mirror, but there was only a giant bullet hole and no glass. She kept driving, her eyes drifting over the dashboard, not wanting to see it, the speedometer dropping, barely thirty-five now.

She was almost at the highway. "Horace! You all right? Horace? Horace!"

There wasn't any answer and there wasn't any time to look. If she stopped to cross the highway—"Aww, shit!" An eighteen wheeler, coming up fast. She held her foot to the floor, almost at the stop sign now, the train growing in the distance along the tracks just beyond.

She hit the horn button for the eighteen wheeler, but the horn didn't work. "Fire your gun, Rufe! Do it!"

"Right!" She heard gunfire drowning out his answer, her ears ringing with it now, a hollowness like being underwater filling her head.

She was into the intersection, the stop sign an ignored blur, the air horn from the eighteen wheeler rising in her perception. She looked right. "Aww—"

She pressed her foot to the pedal but she knew the pedal was already as far down as it would go. "Rufe!"

"Ohh, my God!" She saw a blur at the far right edge of her peripheral vision, felt the impact and heard the screech of the air horn and she had no steering and she brought her arms up in front of her face, her stomach suddenly churning.

The van was rolling and she was pressed against Rudy and Rudy was dead and she screamed.

The van stopped moving. She smelled gasoline.

She opened her eyes.

"Rosie!"

"I'm—I think I'm—"

She tried moving her legs and her left leg didn't move and she started to scream, but then she looked

down—it wasn't down; it was up and that shouldn't be
—and she saw Rudy's dead leg over hers.

She twisted and fell, banging her head against the
roof. She looked beside her. Horace Whitelaw was as
dead looking as Rudy, eyes wide open; except there was
no glass through his throat; only a half-dozen holes in his
chest and blood all over him.

She realized she was crawling, toward the shot-out
windshield. She half fell through, ripping her pants on
the shard of glass.

"Rosie!"

Rose Shepherd saw the train. It was coming, very fast.
She was standing, her whole body trembling.

"Rosie?"

"Here!"

"They're comin', Rosie!" Rufus Burroughs was coming around the side of the van, limping badly. He had
her H & K slung across his back, his Colt AR-15 in his
right fist. "Get across the tracks! Do it!"

She had it back now, whether it was nerve or self-
preservation or a little of each and she grabbed his left
hand and started dragging him. "Come on!"

"I twisted my damn ankle—go on!"

Rose Shepherd threw his left arm across her shoulders and started walking him, looking behind her. The
green van and the blue sedan were about to enter the
intersection; the eighteen wheeler they'd collided with
was jackknifing about a hundred yards down the highway, the driver half falling out. She looked ahead, the
train almost at the crossing. "Come on, Rufus," she said
softly, evenly, just the way her mother had always spoken whenever she or one of her two brothers—Jim was

an accountant in Nashville and Bill a window dresser in Chicago—had been hurt.

"Don't mother me, dammit!"

And he pushed away from her, tears in the corners of his eyes as he walked unaided, limping heavily on his left foot. They were at the tracks. Rose looked back. The blue sedan was into the intersection, a face poking up through the moon roof. In a second, it would be the muzzle of an automatic weapon.

She reached to her right hip, and, despite the flap having been opened earlier, the Commander-sized Detonics Servicemaster was still there. It came into her fist—she was running on ether only now, not really consciously aware—and her left hand was racking back the slide. She stabbed the pistol toward the windshield of the blue sedan and fired twice.

The blue sedan was still coming.

She stopped, inhaled, held the pistol in both her fists —people told her she had small hands but they had always seemed ungainly and large to her. She settled the sights on the face above the moon roof. "Man in the moon, eat shit!"

She fired and the head snapped back, but she didn't hear the sound of the shot, only the train's air horn and Rufus Burroughs's voice. "Get across, Rosie!"

Rose Shepherd looked away from the swerving blue sedan with the crushed fender. She was standing in the middle of the railroad tracks, Rufus Burroughs was reaching for her, the train was almost on her. She jumped left, her left palm and the outside of the fingers of her right hand—she still held the .45 automatic— scraping against the gravel. There was a rush of wind, tearing at her hair and her clothes.

Rufus Burroughs was beside her. "On the train for a while—the only chance—come on!"

She was getting up, boxcars whizzing past her but not moving that fast when she really looked at them. The train had started to slow down; there was a grade here. Rufus Burroughs's hands closed over her pistol, taking it from her, and she heard him shout something over the clack-clack-clack sounds and when she looked up at him his hands were on her waist and she felt as if she were flying and something slammed hard into her and she rolled onto her back.

"We're in deep shit, Rosie," Rufus Burrough shouted, the clack-clack-clack sounds different somehow. They were inside a boxcar. . . .

David Holden was drinking beer because it was that or wine and he didn't like wine that much. All his hard liquor was gone and it was illegal until the emergency passed to buy or sell the stuff. It was a rerun of *Gilligan's Island* and the Skipper was mad at Gilligan but what was so new about that?

Mary Ann's hair, in black and white, looked like Elizabeth's hair and Holden realized he was crying. He lit another cigarette and closed his eyes but the tears still came and he could feel them, rolling down his cheeks.

CHAPTER
21

Rufus Burroughs stood in front of Deputy Commander Ralph Kaminsky's desk, his left ankle screaming at him almost as if it could speak—*Pain!*

"Sergeant Burroughs. I want you to come clean with me."

Burroughs didn't know what to say, so he didn't say it.

"Sergeant Burroughs, there was an automobile traveling on Highway 97 when the incident with the blue van that belonged to Horace Whitelaw took place. You and Detective Shepherd were positively identified. What the hell was the meaning of that? Some kind of damn paramilitary shit or what?"

"Sorry, sir?"

"Burroughs. You and Rudy Goldfarb and Horace Whitelaw were all good friends. What was it you guys were doing? This smells like vigilantism to me."

Rufus Burroughs cleared his throat. "Have you spoken to Detective Shepherd yet, sir?"

"As soon as she gets in. But I'm talking to you now, Burroughs."

Ralph Kaminsky was bald on top and skinny and had weasely black eyes. But it was unfair, as some officers insisted, to say that Kaminsky disliked black people. He disliked everyone. "What do you want to talk about, sir?"

"You and Detective Shepherd were in the van belonging to Detective Whitelaw. I have an eyewitness. I want your badge. I want your gun. I want your confession."

Burroughs didn't say a word.

"I understand there's a whole group within this department and I want names named. The proper procedures will be followed to nail these revolutionaries—"

"They're fuckin' scumbags, Kaminsky."

"They are citizens of the United States and entitled to arrest and all the Miranda rights and due process and everything else, not some damn vigilante justice, Burroughs. This isn't some excuse for a lot of crazy minority cops to run amuck, for God's sake!"

Burroughs looked at him. "Minority?"

"You and Detective Shepherd and Whitelaw and Rudy Goldfarb."

"Okay, already. Rose Shepherd's a woman. Rudy Goldfarb was a Jew. I'm black. What's minority about Horace Whitelaw?"

Kaminsky looked down at his hands. "Maybe for some reason he never mentioned it, but he was a Catholic."

"A Catholic? What the hell's a majority? White? Protestant? What the hell is Kaminsky? You're Polish— that's—"

"I'm not Polish and I'm not Catholic, Burroughs. But this is clearly a minority group thing. And I understand —I really do—why you people are upset, what with this Front for the Liberation of North America proclaiming it represents you—"

"No bunch of Commie killers represent me or any other black person—or any woman or any Catholic or any Jew. They just represent their own damn selves, Kaminsky."

"I'm bringing charges based on the eyewitness account. But if you cooperate, things will go easier on Detective Shepherd and the rest of your fellow conspirators."

Burroughs felt the tension in his voice, his voice trembling, low. "What happened to going after the guilty?"

"I have an eyewitness putting you and Shepherd at the scene of an armed felony. I could give you a list of crimes like leaving the scene of an accident, assault with intent to do bodily harm, unlawful use of a weapon —the state and Federal boys are in on this too. But out of respect to me—to me, Burroughs!—they let me handle the arrest. And you should get down on your knees and—"

"Call you 'massa' or what?"

"That'll be just about enough—"

There was nothing but the truth now, Rufus Burroughs knew. "We were following them. We were all legally armed peace officers. They ambushed us, opened fire, and we fought for our lives—you understand that concept, man?"

"The report of the eyewitness, Burroughs—"

"The only eyewitness was the guy drivin' the damn

eighteen wheeler, sucker. They got a man in the department—right? You?"

"All right." Kaminsky stood up, fingertips against the
desk top, his face livid. "Put your badge and your gun
on the desk—right now, you—"

"What? Nigger?"

"You said it, Burroughs. And you evidently know
what you are. The badge and the gun—now!"

Rufus Burroughs took the badge case out of his
pocket and threw it down on the glass that covered the
top of the desk. The glass didn't crack and he'd wanted
it to.

"Now the gun."

Burroughs reached under his coat.

Kaminsky said, "You're one of these gung-ho types
who carry two—let me see 'em both. Now!"

Rufus Burroughs shrugged his shoulders and took the
four-inch subdued 629 from his right hip, his left hand
reaching to the Bianchi upside-down rig under his left
armpit and ripping the two-and-a-half-inch .38 Special
loaded Smith 66 from the leather. He didn't put the
guns on the desk top, but pointed them at Kaminsky.
"Let's see your gun, shithead!"

Kaminsky's upper lip started to tremble and his left
eye twitched once. "What—what are—"

"On the desk, mother. And right now, shootin' you'd
be the best thing that happened to me all day."

Kaminsky reached under his jacket to his right hip.

Burroughs let himself smile. "Like Dirty Harry says,
huh?" And Burroughs laughed. Kaminsky put the gun
—a glisteningly new looking Detective Special—on the
desk. Burroughs rammed his 629 back into the leather,
picking up the Dick Special, working the cylinder re-

lease catch back, shaking out the department-mandated .38's onto the floor, then kicking them away. He threw the gun onto the leather sofa at the far side of the paneled room. "Take off your jacket, Kaminsky."

"What the—"

"Jacket off or I drop you, man!"

Kaminsky started out of his jacket.

"Now the shoes."

"What are—"

"Shoes, Kaminsky."

Burroughs moved around to the side of the desk. Kaminsky kicked off his shoes.

"Good. Now—open your belt and your fly—want the pants open all the way."

"I will not!"

Burroughs smiled and shoved the gun at Kaminsky's face. Kaminsky obeyed, dropping the belt on the floor, unbuttoning then unzipping his fly. "Now. Hands up high—high as you can reach!"

Kaminsky didn't move.

Burroughs drew the little stainless revolver's hammer back and Kaminsky's hands went up for the ceiling and his pants dropped to his ankles. "That's good, Kaminsky. Now. Just that way—walk me outa the buildin'."

"You're crazy if you think—"

"Maybe I am crazy—all torn up inside with grief. Wanna find out?"

Kaminsky started for the door, his trousers around his ankles, hobbling more than walking. He stopped at the door. "Use your left hand to open the door, then back up over your head. One screw up and I drop you."

"When they catch you—"

"If, asshole," Burroughs hissed.

Kaminsky opened the door, hesitated, then started hobbling through, his boxer shorts on display for all the world to see.

In the office beyond, Kaminsky's pretty blond secretary Laureen turned around in her chair. She dropped a yellow pencil from her hand, her blue eyes wide. And then she brought both hands up over her mouth and started to laugh.

"See—you're a big hit, Ralph. Keep walkin', babes."

Kaminsky kept walking. A police cadet standing beside the water cooler started to laugh, then quickly turned away, red faced. More of the women in the outer office beyond were turning toward them, laughing at Kaminsky. A uniformed cop—Brown or Black or Green or some color name Burroughs couldn't remember— started to draw his revolver. "Tell him to be cool, Kaminsky."

"Holster that gun, man!"

And coming up the corridor just behind the uniformed officer, Burroughs saw Rose Shepherd. She was wearing a gray suit, the skirt midcalf length. Annette had had one—why did women wear such silly things? Burroughs thought absently. Annette—

But the fancy blackened stainless steel .45 Rose Shepherd carried was out of her purse in the next second. "Rufe?"

"Pizza hit the fan, Rosie."

"Aww—"

"Cover my back. We're leavin'. Ralph Kaminsky here decided to help us get out the door."

She visibly shrugged her shoulders, the .45 in her right hand now, her left hand pushing back her jacket and touching at her waist. She started laughing, saying, "You do have gorgeous knees, Ralph."

"Detective Shepherd—talk sense to him! Once you're out this door, there's no turning back."

Burroughs watched her eyes for a moment. She brushed a strand of hair away from her forehead with the back of her left hand, both tiny fists closing on the butt of her .45 then. "Rufe?"

"Some ringer spotted us gettin' away from the Leopards and the guys they were with. He's stickin' us with a rap as long as your arm for defending ourselves."

"Vigilantism, Burroughs! Vigilantism!" Ralph Kaminsky asserted loudly.

"You thought this through, Rufe?" Rose Shepherd asked, her voice almost a whisper.

"This or jail for us while those fuckin' terrorist revolutionaries run around killin' people."

She looked at him for a moment longer, then walked straight up to Kaminsky and put the muzzle of the .45 against the tip of his nose. "You misbehave, little boy, and if Rufe doesn't nail your ass, I will." And she gave Kaminsky a gorgeous smile. She looked at Burroughs. "I'll back you up, Rufe." She crossed around them, the .45 still in both hands.

Burroughs shoved Kaminsky ahead. "Hobble faster, man." It was still a hundred yards to the front door and then they had to get across the street to where he'd parked the car. The corridor beyond the outer office was filling with uniformed cops and plainclothes guys, hands by their guns; but Burroughs had worked with most of them, and once Kaminsky was passed, some shot him a brief smile, others a wink.

But once he and Rosie were in the car and away,

Rufus Burroughs knew, their troubles would really begin. He put such thoughts out of his mind.

"Keep moving," Burroughs snapped.

They were nearly to the large, frosted glass doors that led to the reception area.

"Ralphie—when we get to those doors, open 'em."

"Comin' up behind us! Two of our guys with guns drawn."

"Let 'em know you're serious if you have to, Rosie," Burroughs called back.

"Freeze, guys!" It was Rosie's voice again.

"You won't shoot another cop, Rose!" He recognized the voice—it was the SWAT team commander, O'Brien.

"Try me!"

Burroughs didn't dare look back. They were at the doors. "Catch the door, Ralph. And I'm so close to you, if it weren't for my nicer complexion they'd think we were Siamese twins."

Kaminsky hobbled an extra step, opened the door on the right. Burroughs edged right beside him so they could go through the door together, his cocked revolver at Kaminsky's right temple. "Tell 'em anybody does somethin' heroic, you're dead. Tell 'em!"

"He's going to kill me—don't try anything!" Kaminsky shouted.

There were three cops, all of them young, only two that he knew well enough to recognize, standing in the foyer, revolvers leveled at him. "I'll kill him, guys. I never had any use for this shithead and I'll do it."

"Lower your guns!" Kaminsky shouted.

Burroughs stayed in the middle of the foyer, the safest place. He could cover Rosie and and cover the doors leading to the street at the same time. "Rosie!"

Rose Shepherd called back, "You got me as I come through the door!"

"I got you!"

She backed through the door, the .45 at chest height, a dozen guys just a few feet behind her, half of them SWAT.

It was O'Brien's voice that he heard now. "Neither one of you is taking Kaminsky through that door."

Burroughs snapped back, "He's fuckin' dead if you mess with us, O'Brien."

"And so are you, O'Brien!" Rosie hissed.

"Okay, Ralphie," Burroughs ordered. "Through the door and watch out you don't catch a draft." He prodded Kaminsky ahead. Kaminsky started to stumble, Burroughs catching at him, the three uniformed guys moving fast. But Burroughs moved faster. Burroughs grabbed Kaminsky's left ear and snapped Kaminsky's head back, the muzzle into his right ear. "Don't make me!"

The uniformed officers edged away.

Burroughs pushed Kaminsky ahead, still holding to the man's ear, Kaminsky working the door without being told. And they were out, at the top of the stairs, a dozen uniformed officers, some of them SWAT, at the base of the stairs with M16's, one on each side of the doorway as well, each with a riot shotgun. "Tell 'em to be cool, Kaminsky!"

"Do what he says! He's insane!"

"Yeah, I'm insane all right. Move!" He got Kaminsky to the edge of the top stone step, a dozen, broad and worn, remaining before they reached the sidewalk. A strong, almost hot wind had picked up.

Burroughs risked a glance back.

Rosie backed through the doorway. The instant she was out the wind caught her hair, her clothes, the front of her skirt billowing up from her legs. There was a momentary flash of thigh and black lace, her left hand moving to control her clothes, the muzzle of the .45 never wavering.

Burroughs started Kaminsky down the steps, still holding to Kaminsky's left ear, the gun still at Kaminsky's right. "Come on, Rosie!"

"Right behind you!"

They were halfway down the steps when Rufus saw a flicker of movement and had the instantaneous sick feeling that it was all going bad. One of the SWAT guys moved to jump him. Burroughs dragged Kaminsky back. He started to twist the muzzle of the revolver toward the SWAT man. But then he heard Rosie shouting, "Mason! One more inch! Do it!"

The SWAT man froze. Burroughs dragged Kaminsky closer, Kaminsky starting to fall. Burroughs caught him, Burroughs's left arm around Kaminsky's neck now. Kaminsky was sweating, and with the wind blowing across him, Burroughs could smell body odor mixed with fear. "You keep your head, Ralph, you'll be back in your little office before you know it."

"I'll get you," he snarled through his teeth.

"You hold that thought." They were at the base of the steps now, Rosie at the edge of Burroughs's peripheral vision. For the first time, Burroughs noticed that Rose Shepherd's car was parked a few slots back from his own on the opposite side of the street. "Now," he shouted. "Everybody listen up. O'Brien! Hear me?"

"I hear ya," the SWAT commander called down from the height of the steps.

"This is the way we're playin' it. Rosie gets her car."
She drove a ten-year-old dark-green Mustang with the
same big V-8 interceptor engine in it that the full-sized
police cars used to have. His own wheels were slow-
moving junk. "Then we take Kaminsky for a little ride.
Just use your heads. I have a pistol to Ralphie's head
here for just one reason. I want to get away. As soon as
we're away and gone, Ralphie gets dropped off safe and
sound. Anybody follows us, we see any choppers in the
air, anything phony, you don't get Kaminsky. Close in
on us, Ralphie's brains are all over Rosie's new uphol-
stery. Now. Some of you might think Ralph doesn't have
enough brains to make that much of a mess"—there
was laughter from a few of the officers, the ones who
didn't have their guns drawn—"but let's not find out,
huh?"

"I'm getting the car when you say."

"Now, Rosie!"

She moved past him, covering the same people he
had covered as they crossed body planes.

Then she was in front of the wall of men between her
and the street. And the wall split. She started into the
street. A police car pulled up fast, the Mars lights on.
Two uniformed men jumped out; Rosie crouched, her
pistol leveled between them. "Kaminsky—pull their
plugs now!" Burroughs rammed the revolver's muzzle
against Kaminsky's ear, hard.

"You men! Put down your guns! On the hood of the
car. Step back. Dammit! That's an order!"

The two uniformed cops looked at each other for a
second, then set their revolvers down and stepped
away from them.

Rosie kept going, across the street, fumbling in her

purse one-handed for a few torturous seconds, then she had the door open. There was a throaty growl as the Mustang started up. She eased it into the street. A semi passed, blocking her from view for an instant then was gone. She U-turned in the middle of the street and pulled up just ahead of the police car and the two disarmed men on either side of it. She was out of the car, her pistol across the roof line, aimed up toward the building. "O'Brien! One of your guys twitches and you get it between the eyes. You've shot against me in matches. You know I can do it!"

Burroughs started Kaminsky moving.

They were off the curb, passing the police car. Then they were beside Rose Shepherd's car. "You get him in, Rufe—I'll cover you."

"Open up!" Burroughs ordered. If they were going to try anything, now was when. And if one shot was fired, that would tear it. "Fold the passenger seat forward, man!"

As smoothly as he could, Burroughs put one foot inside, then dragged Kaminsky after him, never moving the muzzle of the gun. It was cramped in the backseat. He let go of Kaminsky's ear, caught at the door, and tugged it closed. "Go for it, Rosie!"

"Remember! Nobody follows us!" She was into the car, the Mustang streaking away before the door was fully closed. Burroughs's eyes were riveted behind them, his thumb slowly lowering the Smith's hammer.

"You signed your own death warrants—both of you," Kaminsky snapped.

"Be cool, Ralphie. Rosie?"

"What?"

"Get your radio on."

"No—my scanning monitor. O'Brien's outfit uses another frequency sometimes."

He could hear the police calls, warning not to intercept.

"What are you going to do with me?"

Burroughs leaned back and looked Kaminsky straight in the eye. "We're gonna drop you as soon as we can. I don't like lookin' at you. And then we'll drop your pants about a mile later on. Get 'em off, Ralphie."

Burroughs heard Rosie start to laugh.

CHAPTER

22

There really was no winter, except for brief cold snaps and rain. Other parts of the United States that usually had heavy snows and bitter cold experienced a milder season as well. Better weather for the killers whom the media called revolutionaries and others called terrorists. The label "revolutionaries" applied only because periodically manifestos laden with standard Communist ideology were left in newspaper machines or taped to pay phones for television commentators to "publish to the people."

The ones the media labeled terrorists called themselves the Patriots and used the very methods of the revolutionaries themselves—quick, brutal hit-and-run attacks, disappearing, resurfacing to strike again. The difference, little emphasized by the media, was all in the targets. The "revolutionaries" of the Front for the Liberation of North America ambushed police cars, bombed bars and other businesses frequented by servicemen, firebombed business districts, made assassination attempts, often successful, against prominent public figures from politics and industry.

The Patriots hit the the FLNA where they met, where they planned, where they hid, where they lived; at least twice (but probably more, since twice was all that was reported in the media) heavy gun-battles broke out between Patriot and FLNA forces.

David Holden realized he had become a cynic, but living in a United States that more and more seemed like Lebanon would do that to anyone, he told himself.

He sat in front of the television set. It was March now and by February he had given up on trying to drown himself in beer.

Hard liquor sales were still banned and so a flourishing business of bootlegged whiskey, gin, vodka, Scotch, and everything else had, of course, established itself. This was common knowledge and almost jokingly reported in the media as well. The prices were inflationary, but it was a sellers' market in the truest sense. The sale of firearms and ammunition had been temporarily banned, and some prominent national politicians called for making the ban permanent. Honest citizens hoping to defend themselves against the escalating violence had turned to bootleggers of a different sort.

Holden had twice encountered persons who whispered of such suppliers and he had avoided any contact, his own ammunition supply adequate to his needs. It was common knowledge that a considerable force of Federal agents were engaged in entrapment operations aimed at apprehending not only the illegal arms dealers but their customers as well. The lion's share of arrests so far had been customers, who were, after all, easier to catch.

The police had brought Holden in twice for questioning since January, asserting that he was in contact with Rufus Burroughs, much-vaunted local leader of the Patriots. But, even with the abrogation of various search-and-seizure rights and the bending of the rules of arrest and evidence in order to "meet the growing crisis," Holden's hidden weapons had not been found and they had been unable to detain him overnight.

The news broadcast was of particular interest to him tonight. The network had videotaped an exclusive interview with one of the local FLNA leaders, a man calling himself only "the Vindicator." Head and face hooded with a black or dark-blue ski mask allowing only the sight of red-ringed eye slits and a slash of a mouth, the Vindicator sat in shadow and spoke with affecting eloquence. "We have not been the ones to initiate violence." Lie. "We have responded to the violence of the oppressive government, confining our targets only to the police and military." Lie. "The so-called 'Patriots' are wholly responsible for the great preponderance of civilian casualties." Lie. "And I cannot blame the people for their outrage against these heavily armed fanatics who are, as secret CIA documents we have uncovered clearly show, controlled and supplied by, and acting on orders of, the United States." Lie.

The documents, of course, could not be revealed at this time.

Holden had reduced his consumption of cigarettes in the last two weeks, having gotten himself up to two packs per day. He was down to half a pack.

Thomas Jefferson University would be reopening soon with a limited class schedule. An insurance policy had paid off (he'd forgotten it existed at the time of the

funeral arrangements) and his money supply was suffi-
cient to live on until paychecks became regular again.

Along with a gradual return toward nonsmoker
status, Holden had started running again. With no family, the three-times-each-week workouts with weights
and the exercise equipment in the basement were now
twice daily.

He avoided giving himself the opportunity to think
about why he was pulling himself up out of the wallow
of despair, because when he thought about it, he realized there was no reason at all and he would have been
better off dead like all the people he had loved.

CHAPTER

23

A phenomenon of the eighties had been the development of a human subspecies known as "mallies." They were fast becoming extinct, Holden realized as he turned the station wagon into the shopping-center parking lot. The huge supermarket was at the far end of the largest shopping center in the entire area, various well-known department and specialty stores, boutique shops, restaurants offering everything from a fast cheeseburger to overpriced, self-proclaimed gourmet meals in abundance. The mall had been a favorite place for Meg to go, Elizabeth too.

But few people ventured from their homes without definite purpose these days, and fewer still let their children wander aimlessly window-shopping and laughing. There was very little laughing at all, anywhere. When the media wasn't full of news of the FLNA or the Patriots or the government enacting new temporary restrictions to confound the revolutionaries (which did nothing more than circumscribe the activi-

ties of the citizenry the government was trying to pro-
tect) there was much talk of the steadily nosediving
economy.

People just weren't buying because they were staying
hidden in their homes. Factories and retail outlets in
areas in or near the violence were closing because employees were too frightened to report for work. There
were already subtle hints of food shortages on the hori-
zon, the shortages from breakdown in supply and distri-
bution. Already, farmers were complaining of falling
prices.

Holden parked the car, looking to right and left, front
and back, to be certain he was unobserved. Everyone
watched everyone these days. Despite the strict regulations against firearms being taken from home or place
of business, Holden had decided that he would never
again travel unarmed unless absolutely necessary. He
had been careful to avoid using any of the major arteries
where random police searches were conducted in the
hope of nabbing FLNAs or Patriots. Satisfied he was not
being watched, Holden took the .45 he had nearly used
to end his life and slipped it under his jacket into the
waistband of his trousers.

He got out of the car and locked it, leaning down to
look through the windows to make certain all other
locks were secured. He was, as yet, undecided about
how he could travel safely back and forth between his
house—it had ceased to be a home—and the university.
There were roadblocks on the main arteries, and to be
caught with a firearm meant immediate arrest and con-
finement without bail until arraignment, which, because of the backlog in the court system, could take
weeks. The jails, overcrowded before the violence had

begun, were reportedly jammed beyond capacity. The gangs that ruled them behind bars were even more brutal. Holden had often wondered if such reports— gang rapes of inmates, beatings, deaths—were merely circulated to make people more reluctant to risk breaking the new regulations, none of which had the true force of law.

Satisfied his car was secure, Holden started inside. The .45 and its single spare magazine was the only weapon he had not hidden semipermanently beneath the floorboards of his recreation room.

He used the mall entrance, the supermarket accessible either that way or directly from the parking lot. Only a few dozen people were in this end of the mall, mostly worried-looking younger women, walking too quickly, one or two of them dragging small children by the hand. A uniformed army sergeant first class stood in the open doorway of the recruiting office, talking with two young men. Salespeople—idle—lingered in the doorways of their shops.

Holden quickened his pace, entering the store itself, and turning right, taking a cart from its row. He'd written a list. He took it out of his pocket. Pasta. Plenty of pasta. It was healthy and he knew how to cook it well enough that it could be eaten, an important consideration these days. Milk, if they had any left. The metro area's largest dairy had been firebombed two weeks ago and milk had been in short supply since. He liked it in his instant coffee because it helped kill the taste.

He started down the aisle.

He'd gone to the grocery store lots of times, either to pick up something Elizabeth specifically needed or accompanying her. But all the decision making, which brand in what quantity at what price, had been done for him. With shortages, much of the decision-making process was obviated at any event.

He stocked up on as much as he could conceivably see safely storing. If the shortages persisted, there would probably be rationing, and hoarding, however antisocial, would prove prudent.

Holden reached the milk freezer. Lots of buttermilk, lots of chocolate milk. He thought about the women he had seen out in the mall and their small children. He could learn to make his instant coffee better. He passed on the milk.

All the less popular types of cheese were in good supply, but they weren't any more popular with him than they were with anyone else. He moved on.

Holden heard the glass shattering first, somehow, and a split second afterward, heard the explosion. And then the screaming started.

Like the dreams he had, all the screaming and the gunfire. He heard gunfire now.

His wife. His daughters. His son. There had been screaming that day.

Holden shoved the cart aside and threw himself into a dead run, more screaming, the sounds of automatic-weapons fire from just beyond the mall entrance. "Out of my way!" Holden shouted, shoving past an old lady and her sparsely filled cart, almost tripping over a red-haired teenage girl in a miniskirt who was standing in the middle of the aisle screaming her lungs out.

Holden reached the checkout lines, people pushing forward, pushing backward, throwing themselves to the floor, screaming, shouting obscenities. He shoved past a man his own age who was shouting "Damn!" over and over again. There was no way around or through. Holden jumped up onto the counter, almost losing his balance, jumped down, pushed past a box boy who was hiding behind the next counter.

The windows fronting the store on the mall side were blown inward and there were at least two people there on the floor in the glass, bloodied, crying for help.

In the mall—he saw them, the black ski masks, the field clothes, the assault rifles, running, firing indiscriminately.

The FLNA.

Holden was through the opening where the glass had been. The recruiting station was in flames, the fire already spread to buildings on both sides. One of the ski-masked gunmen hurled a Molotov cocktail into the open doorway of a toy shop. Holden pulled the .45 from under his jacket. He saw a little child, saw the child's mother run for it, and then the flames sprayed everywhere. Holden's left hand racked the slide of the Colt and he thrust it upward. "You!" The ski-masked gunman who'd tossed the Molotov turned toward him, bringing up his M16.

The .45 in both fists, Holden fired. The FLNAer's body jackknifed as he flipped back, his assault rifle spraying upward, the stained-glass skylight shattering, brightly colored bits of glass falling everywhere around him.

Holden wheeled right. Two of the FLNAers turned toward him. Holden fired once, missing, throwing himself down behind the fountain between the front of the supermarket and the burning toy store. Automatic-weapons fire sprayed up chunks of the bricks bordering the fountain. Holden moved on knees and elbows to the

other side of the fountain. He stabbed the .45 out and
acquired a target, one of the two gunmen firing toward
the fountain.

Holden fired, a double tap. The gunman's body
twitched, his assault rifle falling from his grasp. Holden
fired twice more; the man went down. Holden was up,
running. The second of the two men pivoted, firing at
him as he went. Holden fired his last shot, cursing his
stupidity for not having changed magazines, the second
gunman's body twisted around as he stumbled back,
down but not out. Holden launched himself toward the
first of the two. Holden swapped the .45 into his left
hand and reached with his right, gunfire hammering
into the floor, his hand closing on the M16, his finger
into the trigger guard as he half fell, half rolled back,
spraying a long burst into the second of the two men.
The man's arms flew outward as his body was slapped
back through a plate glass storefront into a group of
mannequins in two-piece bathing suits.

Holden was up, on his knees. Three more of the
FLNAers were in sight, two rushing along in front of the
department store a hundred yards down. Holden shouldered the M16, firing, knocking the legs out from under
one of them. The second man dived to cover. Holden
was up, to his feet. He heard a woman shriek. "Above
you!"

Holden looked up and right. A ski-masked gunman
stabbed a pistol down toward him from the second floor
railing some twenty feet away, and about the same distance up. Holden fired as the FLNAer fired. Holden's
left forearm was alive with pain for an instant, then icy
cold as the realization he'd been shot hit him. The pistol

fell from the FLNAer's hands and the body flopped over the railing and tumbled downward.

Holden's liberated M16 was empty. He moved ahead, sirens low in the distance, barely audible over the crackle of flames and the moaning of the injured.

The first man he'd shot—Holden reached down to him, taking a twenty-round magazine from the man's belt, buttoning out the empty magazine, ramming the fresh one up the M16's magazine well. Holden's left arm was stiffening, the pain intensifying. He let the M16's bolt fly forward, chambering the first round.

He started walking, breaking into a trot, his left arm at his side, the M16 in his right fist.

There was one more. "Come on, motherfucker! Come on out! Scared? Come on!"

He'd seen the remaining one duck for cover into the front of a card-and-gift shop. Holden walked toward it now, glass crunching under his feet.

And then he saw the man, holding a young woman in front of him like a shield. "Don't mess with me, man!" It was a kid's voice. Kids.

"Let her go!"

"Eat shit!"

Holden brought the rifle to his shoulder, his left arm screaming pain as he moved it. The distance was less than ten yards. "You eat it instead." Holden's thumb moved the selector to semi, his right first finger touching the trigger as the girl—a blonde, in her early twenties—screamed. Holden fired.

The FLNAer's head seemed to explode, a wash of blood belching up and back from it, becoming a sick pinkish cloud of spray as the girl fell to her knees screaming and the FLNAer collapsed into a heap.

Holden lowered the rifle, his shoulders slumping. He began to walk, slowly, back toward the fountain. The water was red, the body of a child half fallen into it.

The pain in his arm was making him go light headed. He made the last few paces to the fountain, then sat on its edge, beside the body of the dead child.

There was no more gunfire.

Holden leaned the rifle against his thigh and touched at his arm, a spasm of pain making him see stars for an instant.

The sirens were getting louder.

He told himself to get up. He took the M16 just in case there were more of the FLNAers.

There was an old woman, bleeding, on the floor less than ten feet from him. Holden forced himself to stand, lurched toward her, half falling to his knees. "Ma'am?" Holden put down the rifle.

He raised her head slowly. Her eyes were wide open. Holden thumbed down her lids.

"Freeze, asshole!"

Holden looked around.

Police. Metro.

"No!" A woman came out of the supermarket entrance, clutching a little boy of about six tight against her chest.

The police circled him.

And then they closed with him, clubs coming up, Holden looking up, trying to raise his left arm. But it wouldn't come up fast enough, the club crashing down on his head. He fell, a kick coming for his face as he got his right arm up and tried to roll away.

The woman with the little boy was shouting at them. "Stop it! Stop it! He's a hero! He saved—"

A foot and a club simultaneously and he couldn't block both and there was a flash of light in his eyes and blackness washed over him. . . .

His arm was bandaged—properly, it seemed, as he looked at it—and the stiffness in the right side of his head made him bring his right hand up to his temple. He felt some sort of bandage there too.

Holden was lying on an examining table, he realized, and the coldness of the metal made him realize something else. Under the green paper sheet, he was naked. He saw a face looking down on him, a woman with tired eyes and a hesitant smile. "Don't try to sit up. We had to put you under for the arm wound. It was not critical but deep. The X-rays look pretty good. And you've got a nasty knot on your head. You need to take it easy for a few days just in case of concussion." She started to walk away.

"Hey?"

"I'm Doctor Candler and we're in the infirmary at the Metro emergency command post."

His eyes followed her toward the door. Two uniformed police officers stood there, and as she passed through the doorway and closed the door behind her, one of the cops said, "Get your ass up and get your clothes on. People waitin' to see you."

Holden tried sitting up, and a wave of nausea caught him and he fell back.

"Get up! Now!"

Holden tried again, more slowly. This time it worked. He sat on the edge of the table for a minute, trying to orient himself. The shopping center. The fight. The police. He remembered the woman and her child, the woman shouting that he was a hero. He wondered if this were how heroes were treated today.

He finally stood up, the sheet falling completely away. He realized he wasn't naked, just from the waist up. In the corner, beside a small desk and a drug cabinet, he saw what looked like a pile of rags, presumably his clothes.

Slowly, he started walking toward them. He bent over with difficulty, dizziness coming, passing as he waited for it to, and then he picked up the clothes. His shirt was torn and so was his jacket, the left sleeve all but completely cut away. His left arm was in a sling.

Holden tried getting the jacket on over his right arm, using just his right hand. It wasn't working. One of the cops came over and helped him, none too gently. "Come on, Holden."

At least they knew his name, he thought. He realized his belt was gone. He was wearing his socks, but no shoes. He saw his shoes, track shoes but with the laces removed. He stuffed his feet into them. The soles had been cut apart, as though his captors had been searching for something. It was hard walking in them, but he realized he was walking.

No wallet.

"Where's my stuff?" His voice sounded rough and weak at the same time to him.

"Shut up and keep movin'."

They went through the doorway, a cop on each side of him, then started up a corridor, green and gray, that seemed to go on forever.

Caught with his .45. That was it. Even though he'd nailed some of the FLNAers, they were going to throw him in jail for a few weeks until he came up for arraignment. "Shit," he whispered.

"Keep walkin'."

The walk stopped after what really did seem like forever and one of the cops opened a cheap-looking door and the other gently enough shoved him ahead.

He recognized no one. Two men in shirt-sleeves and half-mast ties, one white and the other Japanese, a third man—an Army captain—in starched fatigues and spit-shined boots, the Japanese pacing the floor, the Army man staring out the venetian-blinded window, the third man perched on the corner of a desk.

There was a chair opposite the desk and Holden was pushed down into it. The man on the edge of the desk nodded and the two cops left. Holden looked around after he heard the door slam shut.

"Doctor David Holden. Correct?"

Holden looked at the man on the edge of the desk more closely. Thinning blond hair, a weary look in his eyes such as everyone seemed to have these days. There was a shoulder holster and his shirt was sweat ringed around it.

"Correct?" the man repeated.

"Correct."

"You're in deep trouble, Doctor Holden. We've got you for everything from unlawful use of a weapon to assault with intent to kill and a half-dozen or so counts of homicide. They're back to giving the death penalty, you know. But if you come clean about Rufus Burroughs, Rose Shepherd, and the rest of their fanatics, we'll listen to some plea bargaining. Otherwise, it's the max for all of it and if you don't get fried in the electric chair, you'll be getting your ass reamed in federal prisons for the rest of your life. You have no choice."

Holden closed his eyes. The doctor had warned him he might have a concussion. He had fainted back there and this was a nightmare or something.

"Holden! Don't pull that sick shit with us!" It was a new voice and Holden opened his eyes. The Army captain was leaning over him. He had bad breath. "You can tell us what we want to know and you're going to, mister."

Nausea.

Holden doubled forward and retched, the Army captain hollering, "God Almighty! My boots!" The smell. Holden felt faint. He leaned back and the faintness increased.

"Get somebody in here." It was the first voice. He let his head sag forward, despite the smell between his legs, and lowered his head.

He heard a door open and slam, then open and slam shut again, then saw a mop and a bucket. He closed his eyes.

Sounds that didn't mean anything because he didn't care. This couldn't be happening. Voices, doors slamming.

"Holden!"

He opened his eyes. It was the man with the sweat-stained shirt and the shoulder holster again. "Tell us about Rufus Burroughs."

Holden mentally shrugged. He'd told the story so often before. "He was the husband of one of my most promising graduate students. I got to know him. I went to two meetings where there were a bunch of cops and veterans. They expressed legitimate concerns about the way the FLNA thing was being handled."

"How could they have know who it was?"

"They didn't, then. I guess. The bombings and stuff. I was only introduced to one person whose name I remember. That was a woman named Shepherd. I guess it was the same Rose Shepherd they talk about on television. Rufus Burroughs was a good guy. He still is. I guess she is too. Burroughs's wife was killed when my wife and children—when they—"

"Burroughs is a violent lunatic. And you work with him, Holden. Either spill everything you know or you're taking the big one."

"How'd you like me to take a pocket knife and start playing with that left arm of yours, asshole?"

Holden looked at the Army captain. The Japanese spoke for the first time Holden noticed. "Captain, you know you can't do that. This is an FBI matter, so stay out of it," and then he went back to pacing.

The other man spoke. "Tell us about the Patriots."

"All I know is what I hear on the news. Sounds to me like they are patriots, just trying to pull the plug on these FLNA bastards."

"Tell us about the Patriots or maybe I'll let Captain Leidecker do what he talked about."

"Jim! For God's sake!"

"Let me handle this, Akiro, huh?" And then he stood up right in front of Holden. Holden looked up. "You talk now. No more fuckin' around."

"Why aren't you out after the bad guys?"

The fist came faster than Holden could move just now. He was falling out of the chair and tasted blood in his mouth and his head ached worse than anything he had felt in his life. He tried to stand up. The Japanese helped him up and back into the chair. Holden spit blood onto the floor, grateful he wasn't spitting teeth. "I want a lawyer."

"You'll get shit."

"I want a lawyer, man!"

The man with the sweat stains turned away, smashing his fist into the palm of his hand.

The Japanese walked over to the desk and picked up a telephone. "This is Wakazashi. Let's get Holden out of here to Detention Center Four and put him in the interrogation unit." He hung up the phone. He looked at Holden. "I realize how the deaths of your loved ones could have embittered you, but the government has the situation in hand. You have to believe that. Burroughs and his people are killers. Nothing more. Private citizens can't go taking the law into their own hands, shooting up the streets. People who do have to be locked up."

"Unless they're FLNA?" Holden snapped.

"You'll be treated humanely but you will tell us what we have to know. Drug therapy. I'm sorry," Wakazashi concluded, as though he hadn't heard what Holden had asked.

"How many more people have to die—like those people in the shopping center—until you have everything under control?"

"That's a ridiculous question, Doctor Holden. We might have had the situation under control by now if we didn't have to waste so much manpower and time and so many other resources going after Burroughs and the nutballs like him."

"If you went after the revolutionaries half as hard,

Burroughs and his 'nutballs' would be out of a job, wouldn't they?"

"We expect a break in our investigation of the FLNA shortly. They'll be rounded up. The biggest problem we have to cope with is the violence caused by these self-styled vigilantes who won't let the proper authorities get the job done."

"You expect me to believe that? Would you?"

The Japanese didn't say anything, just turned away.

Holden heard the door open. It was the two cops again and they hauled him up out of his chair and pro-pelled him toward the doorway. Holden shouted back, "Would you?"

The door slammed. . . .

In the back of the police detention van there were four other men. All of them had shackles on their ankles and thin chains around their waists, their handcuffs at-tached to the chains. Only Holden was slightly freer, his left wrist left unmanacled, presumably because his left arm was bandaged and in a sling. It was very hot inside the van. And wherever Detention Center Four was, it had to be far away because the ride seemed intermina-ble. Holden fell into talking with the oldest of the four men. He was tired looking and about sixty. "What'd you do?"

The man, balding, what hair was left white, looked down at his feet, at his hands. "The hell with it! I had to work. My shop is downtown and the revolutionaries have attacked there so many times hardly anybody comes to buy. We don't have some pension. My wife and me. We go early in the morning to work and come home late. I carried my gun with me because one time we almost got caught right in the middle of it when there was an attack. Shooting. Throwing bottles of gasoline that explode. All the dying. It's all right for me. I still run pretty good. But Sadie's no good running. Her legs. The arthritis. There was a search. You know the kind?"

"Random thing on the streets?"

"The army stopped my car and they found my gun. It's like when the Nazis came in Warsaw. I don't know what my Sadie does, now." The old man started to cry.

Holden started to reach out to touch the old man's shoulder, but his good hand was shackled.

If he had known anything about Rufus Burroughs and the Patriots he wouldn't have told those men in the office, or anyone.

Burroughs had been right, Holden realized now. He wondered if he had realized it earlier, but been too stubborn to admit it?

The van lurched violently, the old man was thrown against him. Then suddenly it stopped, Holden and the old man pitched to the floor.

Automatic weapons fire, light enough to be submachine guns. Glass broke, but nothing Holden could see. Maybe a headlight.

"My God!" the old man whispered. The two younger black men across from Holden began twisting and pulling frantically at their shackles. The fourth man—about Holden's own age and sitting all throughout the drive just staring mindlessly—seemed unchanged.

Holden got to his feet. If these were FLNA . . . But maybe the rear doors would be opened and he could try to make a break for it. He looked at the old man as he helped him back into a sitting position. Could he leave the man behind? There were two guards, only. How many FLNA? Holden began flexing his left hand. At least it was free. If he could grab a gun . . .

As he looked forward through the grill which separated the prisoner transfer compartment from the cab, he saw the two police officers getting out.

He heard the cab doors slamming. A second later, heard keys being turned in a lock.

The police van's rear doors opened.

Holden turned toward the van doors, looking about the compartment for anything he could pick up and use as a weapon.

Through the open doors he saw men in full battle gear, automatic weapons in their hands, the two police surrounded by them. Then there was a face at the door.

The face belonged to Rufus Burroughs.

CHAPTER

24

"So, when we heard what happened, I sort of figured you'd be wanting these." Rufus Burroughs threw a faded green tarpaulin halfway back across the length of a long wooden table.

David Holden reached out to the table. His hand closed over the Defender knife. His guns, his ammunition, his holsters, his web gear, all the things he had secreted beneath the floor boards of the recreation room.

"How did you find this stuff?"

Burroughs grinned. "I worked burglary for three years. You learn to notice where people stash things they don't want found. I had a few anxious minutes, but I asked myself where I'd hide the stuff if I wanted it safe and didn't want somebody noticing me burying it. All the rest of the rooms in the house had either wall-to-wall carpeting or linoleum. But the recreation room had an Oriental rug—"

"It was a fake," Holden almost whispered.

"Rosie and I rolled back the rug, but not for dancin'."
Burroughs grinned again. "I could see where some of
the boards had been pried up and nailed back, so I pried
'em up. There they were. I figured you might want
these too," and Burroughs threw the tarp back the rest
of the way.

Holden set down his knife. The photographs of his
wife and his children, the photo albums, the little construction-paper card Irene had made that he'd left
magneted to the refrigerator all these months.

Holden faced Burroughs, his right arm folding
around him. "Thank you. You'll never know how
much."

"I don't think we're ever goin' back. That's why I took
'em, David."

Holden couldn't speak. He nodded his head. There
was no going back.

All his personal effects, except his .45 and the spare
magazine, had been in a plastic property bag in the
front of the police van. And suddenly, he reached his
hand into his front pocket and took out his keys.

"They impounded your car, David."

"No." Holden stared at the safety deposit key, tossed
the key ring in his hands once, then clenched his fist
tight. . . .

David Holden normally didn't part his hair at all, but
he parted it on the right now. He had planned it out
while the others had slept. Rufus Burroughs had thrown
some clothes into a couple of suitcases for him. Among
them was a tweed sport coat, a pair of dress slacks, and a
pair of loafers.

No one would expect him to surface so soon, he told himself.

"Where are you going?"

Holden looked at her face past his own reflection in the mirror. "I'm picking up something. Rufus knows about it."

"You're crazy," Rose Shepherd said flatly. "You think parting your hair and putting your injured arm into that jacket's going to make any difference?"

"All I have to do is walk into a bank."

"Why don't you walk into Metro Central while you're at it? After all the trouble Rufus went to, you could at least try to stay alive, for God's sake." And she walked away, angry, he supposed.

Holden looked at himself once more in the mirror.

The beard he'd grown because he'd been too lazy to shave for a long while then left because he liked it was gone now, except for the mustache. He looked stupid with it and would shave it off, if he lived that long.

He shrugged his shoulders and picked up the larger of the two Berettas and slipped it under his jacket in the small of his back, the shoulder holster on under his coat, the smaller Beretta already in place, as was the Defender knife.

Holden started across the converted dining room, picking his way over the rolled-up blankets and sleeping bags. Every room in the old farmhouse was converted to a dormitorylike bedroom to house the Patriots, except the kitchen, which was still a kitchen and the living room—from the age of the house it would have been built as a parlor—which served as Rufus Burroughs's office and briefing room.

Burroughs himself had elected to drive, Holden saying he could drive himself, Burroughs insisting. "You tried savin' my wife's life. I don't consider us even yet" was all he had said.

Holden stepped out onto the porch. Twenty-five miles from the city, down a spider web of country roads, the house and the small farm surrounding it were remote enough to seem peaceful.

He heard the screen door slam behind him and turned around with a start. It was Rose Shepherd, changed to a blue denim skirt and a sweater that looked big enough to have fitted two women. "I'm going with." That was all she said, and she walked across the porch, down the three porch steps, and into the dirt-and-gravel driveway, tapping her booted right foot, arms folded across her chest, a large black leather bag slung from her right shoulder. He imagined she carried a gun in it.

A Buick station wagon pulled up from the direction of the nearest of the two barns, Rufus Burroughs at the wheel. Rose Shepherd started into the backseat. Holden reached to close her door with his left arm, realizing his mistake after he made it, the pain going through him like an electric shock. "You're really going to fool them, all right," she snapped, reaching her right hand out and slamming the door closed herself.

Holden climbed into the front seat, Burroughs getting the car into motion before he had the door closed. "How'd you find this place?" Holden asked by way of making conversation.

"Easy enough. We've got a lot of friends, David. Police, military, even some FBI. We did the normal thing you do when you go looking for property. We found ourselves a real estate man. So far, it's been perfect out here. So many little roads leading in and out, we've never been followed yet and we've got plenty of escape routes."

"The way the press talks . . ." Holden started to say. "So much for that."

"Just a few isolated lunatics runnin' around killin' people?" Burroughs laughed. "No. Patriot groups are all over the country, and fighting all over the country. This thing is big. Tell him, Rosie."

She cleared her throat, Holden turning around in his seat to look back at her. "All right. Rufus trusts you enough to tell you everything, I guess I may as well too. Fine. We have a pretty elaborate intelligence network. It's still in its fledgling stages, but it gives us some good information when we need it."

"We don't have an overall leader. Each Patriots group is independent. Works for now," Burroughs added.

"But even though we don't have one central leadership, we swap information; once or twice we've even gotten together with a Patriots group in another area to hit a big target. That FLNA group that got wiped out three weeks ago in Asheville?"

"No—it wasn't in the news, or I missed it," Holden told them.

"Well, that was us and them," Burroughs said.

"We've pieced together a pretty good profile of the enemy forces," Rose Shepherd continued. "Early on in the thing, most of them were fighting gangs from the streets. But once it got rolling, a lot of the older dissident groups, people disaffected with the political system in this country, like that. Well, they joined up. There seems to be a pattern. Some adult—American it seems, but could be a clever ringer—but some adult comes into an area, finds out which are the strongest and best of the fighting gangs, and pitches them. Probably talks about money, power, waste the system, like that. Works them for a while independently, then brings in overseas professionals as advisors. We don't have enough information to make a profile yet, but it's a good bet they're terrorists from Europe and the Middle East. Then the initial recruiter moves on. After a while, the original units are unified under a central command. The FLNA has a serious network and it's growing every day. You'd be surprised at some of the people who are helping them. Or maybe you wouldn't."

"What do you mean?" Holden asked her.

"We just learned one of your old colleagues—that's the term?" Burroughs asked.

Holden nodded. "Yeah."

"A man named Humphrey Hodges. He's dropped out of sight and there is every reason to believe he's working as an advisor for the FLNA. FBI reports I've seen indicate he may have been working in this thing before the violence even started."

Holden realized he shouldn't have been surprised, but he was.

"Women have a right to be curious. What's so important you have to risk your life and ours to go to the bank? You couldn't have that much money as a teacher."

"You're right, there," Holden agreed. "I don't know what it is."

Burroughs just started to laugh. . . .

David Holden lit a cigarette—another prop—and got out of the car, opening Rose Shepherd's door as well.

Rufus Burroughs had suggested it. "They're looking for one man, not a man and a woman. And Rosie can back you up."

She wore a pretty floral print silk scarf over her hair, tied under her chin, and a pair of eyeglasses. As he helped her from the car, Holden asked, "Are the glasses for real?"

"For reading and television. I haven't gotten much chance to use them lately."

They started across the street, Holden more self-conscious than he had ever felt before in his life. He saw a man who looked like the old man from the police van; they had "sprung" him along with the rest of the prisoners, released them to go their way. Suppose it should be the old man and he spoke? The man turned, and it wasn't his face at all.

They reached the curb in front of First Liberty. Holden looked both ways as he opened the door for Rose Shepherd to enter ahead of him. She smiled, passed through the doorway, and he followed her. There was canned elevator music playing in the barely audible range, making it even more annoying.

She waited to follow his lead and Holden inhaled, controlling his breathing, then stopped before the gleamingly polished receptionist desk.

"I'd like to see Paul Henderson, please."

The woman's smile faded. "He's ahh—Mr. Henderson was killed three weeks ago. Did—ahh—did you have an appointment?"

Holden didn't know what to say.

"My husband's at a loss for words, I'm afraid," Rose Shepherd said.

She was good. She was very good. As she said the

word *husband,* she slipped her left hand into a side pocket of her skirt so the receptionist wouldn't notice the absence of a wedding ring.

Holden cleared his throat. Tom had told him something. He tried to remember what. He remembered. "Then I'd like to speak with whoever took over Mr. Henderson's functions here. Is the person in?"

"That's Mrs. Hollings."

"Fine. Then I'd like to see Mrs. Hollings."

"Whom, ahh—"

His name had been on the news broadcasts the previous night and this morning. "Tell her, please, that I'm Thomas Ashbrooke, a friend of Mr. Henderson."

His eyes caught Rose Shepherd's eyes.

The receptionist said she'd tell Mrs. Hollings, then used a telephone, spoke, he guessed, with this Mrs. Hollings's secretary, then put down the receiver.

"Mrs. Hollings will be with you in just a moment if you'd like to have a seat over there by the windows."

Holden looked toward the windows. Anyone walking along the sidewalk could have spotted him. "I'll stand, thanks. Been sitting all day," he told her, remembering his cigarette suddenly, looking around for an ashtray.

He looked at Rose Shepherd. "Well, darling—how about a snack or something after we're through here?" Holden suggested, making small talk for the benefit of the receptionist.

Rose smiled. "Ohh, I don't know, Tom," she began, using the name he'd given the receptionist. "The children and all. All right. But we'll have to be quick."

"Right."

"Mr. Ashbrooke?"

Holden turned around toward the voice—too

quickly, he knew. A woman somewhere in her forties or early fifties, very pretty, extended her hand. "Yes."

"I'm Martha Hollings. How may I help you?"

"Could we speak in your office, please?"

"Yes—of course, Mr. Ashbrooke. Is this Mrs. Ashbrooke?"

"Yes."

Rose took Martha Hollings's hand, "Hi—I'm pleased to meet you."

The two women smiled at each other. Holden felt as if he were going to wet his pants. He didn't. He took Rose Shepherd's elbow and followed Mrs. Hollings across the lobby to a nicely paneled office at the rear. She closed the door and went around to her desk. "How may I help you? Please sit down."

Holden sat. Rose stood by the door, smiling still.

"Did you inherit a great deal of paperwork from Mr. Henderson?"

"Ohh, yes. It was so sudden, of course. Why do you ask? Was it about a loan?"

"No, ahh—I have this key." Holden took his key ring from his pocket and put it on the desk between them.

"That's a safety-deposit-box key. One of the older ones."

"I was told I could present this key and get into the box. That Mr. Henderson would arrange it. And if something were to happen to him, there'd be something in his paperwork to guarantee that I still could."

She smiled. "Well, there's no problem, because all you have to do is sign and of course—"

"That's—" Holden started. He heard a snapping sound and looked toward the door. Rose Shepherd's right hand held a small, stainless steel revolver. He didn't know where it had come from. He guessed under the sweater.

Martha Hollings inhaled audibly. "You're that Professor Holden they're looking for."

"Right, lady," Rose Shepherd snapped. "Let him into his box."

"I can't—"

"Look," Holden told her, standing up, picking up his keys. "Thomas Ashbrooke is my father-in-law."

Her gray eyes flickered toward Rose beside the door. "No," Holden told her. "This woman is a friend. My wife was killed during the attack on Thomas Jefferson University, where I'm a professor—was. There's something my father-in-law left for me in the keeping of Paul Henderson and I don't know what it is. There was supposed to be something in your paperwork that would tell you what to do. I'm sorry. But I have to get into the box. All that stuff they said on the news. It's all lies. I was just trying to save some lives yesterday. That's all."

His head was starting to ache where his right temple was bandaged. "Was Paul Henderson killed by the revolutionaries, the FLNA?"

Martha Hollings nodded. "Yes."

"Was Paul Henderson your friend?"

She laughed. "No. He was the most chauvinistic man I ever met. He did everything he could to keep women out of positions of responsibility here. No. He wasn't my friend." Holden's heart sank. "But no man should be gunned down when he's sitting in a restaurant eating his lunch. I'll take your key. But if anyone says anything, she—with the gun—she forced me to."

Holden looked at Rose. Rose's right hand went into her pocket, the gun in her fist.

Martha Hollings started from her desk, crossed the room, passed through the doorway, Holden and Rose Shepherd following her. She stopped at a rear desk. "I need access to a box for a special customer. Give me your keys, Jean."

"Yes, Mrs. Hollings."

The woman at the reception desk gave her a ring of keys and Martha Hollings turned toward an open vault door. Holden and Rose Shepherd followed her.

Martha Hollings consulted the number on the key Holden had given her. She pulled a tray of yellow index cards out of a three-foot-high file of trays and she whispered, "Pretend you're signing here, Professor Holden."

He took the pen she offered and wrote *Bugs Bunny* on the card.

She closed the file, then marched off into a side room. There had been safety deposit boxes surrounding the file cabinet, but those were modern looking. The boxes here seemed considerably older. "It's one of the big ones, just above my head." She put his key in and hers, twisting them both, the door swinging open. "You'll have to get it. I'm not tall enough."

Holden reached up and started to draw the box out. It was heavy, but not inordinately. There was a hasp for placing a personal lock on the box, but no lock in place. Holden set the box on the table.

Martha Hollings stepped back.

Holden lifted the lid. "Wow."

Rose Shepherd stood beside him. "Holy shit!"

Martha Hollings said, "You'll need a bag. Do you trust me to get it?"

Holden looked away from the contents for a second, looked at Martha Hollings. "Do I have choice?"

"No. Not really. You'd look awfully damn conspicuous carrying it all out in your bare hands."

She walked out, the click of her heels ebbing as he looked back at the open box. "They're all twenties," Rose Shepherd said, riffling a stack of it. "All from fifteen years ago or better. How long were you married?"

"Almost fifteen years," he told her.

And she picked up the pistol placed on top of the stacks of money. "There's something funny about this P-thirty-eight. The weight." She removed the magazine, checked the chamber; both were empty. "It's too heavy. It's got a steel frame. And look here."

Holden took the gun from her hands. There were proof marks with an eagle and a swastika. "That's a wartime gun," she almost whispered.

Holden turned the pistol over in his hands. It seemed sound, despite its apparent age. He looked back at the box. He had never been that good at guessing games. But it looked like well over a hundred thousand dollars in twenty dollar bills, and with them, two spare magazines for the Walther and a box of European-origin 9mm Parabellum hardball. Underneath the box of ammunition there was a large manila envelope. He took the envelope, but refrained from opening it as yet.

"What was your father-in-law into? The money looks syndicate. The gun—I don't know what."

Holden turned toward the entrance, but it was Martha Hollings, returning alone, in her hands two off-white canvas shopping bags, the legend on each bag reading, FIRST LIBERTY'S MY BANK!! She handed him the bags. "They were left over from a promotion we had a few months ago. The best I could do. Can I help?"

He handed her a bag, Rose took the other one, and the two women began to neatly stack the money into the bags. Maybe it was more than a hundred thousand, he realized. He took the Walther and the spare magazines, stuffing them into the side of one of the bags, the box of ammunition into the other.

Holden stepped away from Rose Shepherd and the woman from the bank. He opened the flap of the envelope; nothing was written on the outside.

There was a letter. Holden unfolded it.

Dear Liz and David,

To save you counting it, there's a quarter of a million dollars here.

Get back up off the floor and keep reading.

When you were a little girl, Liz, sometimes you'd ask me how we'd gotten rich. Which I'd thought was very clever of you, because most children would have just taken it for granted. I told you that I worked very hard for the money we had. That's just as true now as when I told you then. But I never told you what I did to earn it.

If you're reading this, I'm either dead and you've inherited the contents of the box or there is some trouble and I've directed you to open it.

I was just a kid in 1930. A little shaver. My family was dirt poor, but whose family wasn't? A rhetorical question? Not really. Because there's an answer. The families of the bootleggers weren't poor at all. So, I got a job helping to unload trucks, watching out for the Feds (we owned enough of the local cops in those days) and I made some money. It was pretty harmless because the bootlegger I worked for only sold the real stuff, not the stuff guys made in their bathtubs with wood alcohol that got you blind or dead when you drank it.

I learned then that supplying people with things they really needed and couldn't get through ordinary channels was where the money was. When Roosevelt got in, Prohibition went out and so did my job. I didn't want to go to school and I was used to having a little money. One of the guys I'd worked with took a shine to me. His name was Pete. Pete had smuggled guns into Mexico before World War I and there were still places that needed the kinds of things he could supply. And again, it went to the people who really needed it. I didn't go home. I went with Pete.

It wasn't long after that when we were smuggling guns into Spain. Pete stopped a bullet. I kept the business going. Everybody knew war was inevitable, a world war again. I made a lot of money and when the war came, I went back home to enlist. But by that time, my reputation had preceded me. I joined the Army. I was "volunteered" for the OSS, the wartime version of the CIA, called the Office of Strategic Services, because we went behind enemy lines and did special things nobody else could. With all the contacts I'd made before the war, and speaking several languages fluently enough to pass for a native when it was that or getting shot, I was what they called a "natural."

With what I learned during the war and my knowledge of arms sales, I was able to turn dimes into dollars once Europe was pacified. So, I did, using the money I'd earned before the war.

By the time you came along, Liz, I was getting out of the business anyway. I invested wisely and legitimately, but I decided that some of the cash I had might someday prove useful as cash or liquid assets. There are numbered accounts in Switzerland. If you did learn about this box from my will, you have the numbers. Diamonds, other precious commodities. You're richer than the will indicated, at least by ten times.

And this is especially for you, David. I know you don't like me much. Too bad. I didn't think a hell of a lot of you either to begin with. But all this money and everything else. It's Liz's by right, and as her husband, yours too. The world is going to hell. You're the historian. You should be able to see that. And just before it hits bottom and you smell the sulphur, you might need to bail out. Consider this a parachute.

Also for David—the gun is a Walther P-38 I took off an SS captain in 1942. It's probably sounder than these dollars.

Love,
Dad

Holden folded the letter closed, replaced it in the envelope.

"You ready?" Rose Shepherd asked him.

"Yeah." Holden looked at Mrs. Hollings. "Thank you."

"It's not from selling drugs, is it?"

"No. Nothing like that. Kind of a wedding present for a rainy day. It's raining outside. Heavily."

"What?" Martha Hollings asked, a puzzled look on her face.

But Rose Shepherd looked at him and smiled.

CHAPTER

25

By the time they returned to the farmhouse, his arm hurt so badly that he could barely sit still in the passenger seat. He went into the house immediately, getting a shot of something for it from the nurse who was one of the Patriot band. The shot made him drowsy and he unrolled his sleeping bag and slept.

He dreamed. He saw Liz and Meg, both of them shielding little Irene with their bodies, Dave going after the killer, then dying himself.

Holden awoke, went into the bathroom, urinated, and then washed his face with cold water, his arm aching badly, stiff from sleeping. There was whiskey in the kitchen, and he needed a drink more than he had ever needed one in his life except that first time back at the house when he'd almost shot himself.

There was an oil lamp burning in the center of the kitchen table and Rose Shepherd, a blanket around her shoulders, sat alone at the table. There was a bottle of whiskey out already and she had a glass.

"I'm sorry," Holden started to say.

"You want a drink?"

He noticed a fancy-looking black .45 on the table.

"Sure. I'll join you."

"The glass isn't mine. Somebody's, but not mine. Fresh glasses on the drainboard by the sink. Get me one?"

"Sure." Holden got two glasses, pushed the used one away, and poured them each a shot. "Nice looking .45."

"Detonics Servicemaster. Same size as a Commander. It's a black oxide finish over the stainless steel. Makes it look kind of worn, but shiny guns can get you killed in an alley."

"What about that other shiny gun of yours?"

"The Sixty? That's for hard times, usually. If I pull it, I shoot it. So it can be as shiny as anything. I don't care. What do you care about?"

"What?" Holden lit a cigarette. There was an empty ashtray on the table. Apparently the mysterious secret drinker wasn't a smoker.

"Are you here hiding, or helping? That's a lot of money. You could buy your way out of the country and into a new life with it, David."

"I know that."

"So? What's it going to be?"

"I'm tired."

"We're all tired," she said. "I'm one of the lucky ones. I'm not married, don't have kids. Most of them do or did. Patsy Alfredi—the woman who gave you the shot for your arm?"

"Yeah?"

"Her husband and son got it. Her husband was a cop and the FLNA ambushed him and his partner. Her son was in the Air Force and the bar he was in was firebombed."

"God bless her," Holden murmured, drinking a little of his whiskey.

"Yeah. I suppose. Maybe you should get out. I don't think we're going to win, sometimes," and she swallowed half of her drink. "If we do win, they're not going to amnesty us. We'll be on the run forever."

"That's a long time. It's a funny word that only means something to lucky people," Holden told her.

"What?"

"Liz and I—we used to say 'forever' a lot."

"Look—ahh—Rufe told me all of what went on. So, maybe I know too much about you."

Holden couldn't think of anything to say. She took his cigarette from his fingers and dragged on it, then handed it back. "When are you going to make up your mind?"

"I'm staying. I don't have any reason to do anything else. Maybe I want some revenge."

"Then get out of here first thing in the morning," she said, shaking her head, sipping at her drink. "You'll not only get yourself killed, but you'll take a lot of good people with you."

"You the chaplain?" Holden smiled.

"No. I haven't figured out what I am yet. Except an insomniac sometimes. Arm hurting you?"

"Yeah," he told her.

"I'm sorry. About everything," and she got up and left.

Holden sat there for a while, finishing his drink.

CHAPTER
26

Rufus Burroughs sat at the card table that was his makeshift desk. "I've gotten some word through those kids who helped us about a month ago when the FLNA was gonna steal that painter's grade aluminum compound."

"Bombs?" Holden interrupted without thinking.

"That's right, David. But you know all those improvised demolitions things, right? From the SEALs?"

Holden shrugged his shoulders and it made his left arm hurt. Rose Shepherd had avoided him all day, even walked out of the room once when he entered. But she was here now, looking at him. He looked back at her. "I thought you knew that."

"No. I didn't know that."

Burroughs said, "Am I interruptin' somethin'? Anyway. These are good kids. You look at all the punks in with the FLNA and you start thinkin' things you shouldn't. I know I was for a while. So, they tell us there's a nest over on Eighth and Kirkpatrick, right under Metro's nose. The stuff was relayed by one of the usual routes. I know it's good."

"Can't you tell the cops?" Holden interrupted. "Look, man—I'm—"

"No. You have a right to know that regardless of what you do, David," Burroughs said. "Like I told you. We have a lot of people on our side. Kids, old people, cops, truck drivers, cabbies, teachers. Some Feds, some military, even some military police. When we first started doing this, we looked back on the thing that got Rosie and me nailed in the first place, David. So, we figured goin' after the bad guys ourselves wasn't such a hot idea. Why not just get the leads and try to feed them to the FBI or the cops we could trust on Metro or other departments? The FLNA owns people, David. If they act on the tip at all, they either fart around so much that by the time they move the tip's no good, or they move fast and somebody's tipped the FLNA and they've pulled out. We can't trust the authorities, man. I wish it weren't that way."

"Are you in, David, or out?"

Holden turned and looked at Rose Shepherd.

"If you're in, you're in. If you're not, you don't have any business listening to this. None at all, David."

Holden watched her for a moment longer.

He heard Rufus Burroughs talking, but still watched Rose Shepherd. "David—we can use men with training like you had in the SEALs. A lot of us are cops, a lot of us are veterans. But guys with special warfare training are pretty scarce."

Holden looked away from Rose Shepherd, looking at Rufus Burroughs. "I almost got myself killed back in the shopping center, for God's sake. I'm no good to you for anything like that. I'll fight. But—"

"What?"

Holden looked at Rose Shepherd. "I'm in, I said."

Rufus Burroughs stood up and crossed the room, shoved his ham-sized hand toward Holden and said, "It's like ridin' a bicycle, David. It'll come back to you."

Holden shook his hand.

Others in the room extended their hands and he took them.

He looked at Rose Shepherd. She was looking back.

Rufus Burroughs started talking again. "We need to hit this nest. That whole area around Eighth and Kirkpatrick was firebombed about a month ago. So they're using one of the sealed-off buildings. The kids who came up with the information think they store weapons and shit there and use it like a staging area for attacks in the Metro area. If they're right, we could put a real crimp in their plans for a while if we hit it hard enough. We need to do it tonight. Rose—you worked that area a couple of years back when you were in uniform, right?"

"Yeah," she said.

"You can guide us in?"

"Yeah."

"Everybody grab some dinner. Gonna be a long night. David. You sit this one out. That arm of yours."

"I shoot okay with the other hand," Holden told him.

Burroughs nodded. "So be it, my man." Burroughs left the room, the others following.

Holden started to leave, too, then felt a hand at his good arm. He turned around. It was Rose Shepherd. "What?"

"You've been calling me Rose," she said evenly, almost quietly.

"What do you want me to call you?"

"People I care about call me Rosie." She walked out of the room.

David Holden just stood there. . . .

Seven of them would go, one of them staying with the vehicle, six actually hitting the "nest," as Rufus Burroughs called it.

And they geared up in the dining room/bedroom now.

Black battle dress utilities were a sort of uniform for the Patriots. Sewn on the left jacket sleeve just below the shoulder, like a unit patch, was an American flag.

David Holden pulled on his jacket. There had been a good array of sizes to draw from and the BDUs were a good fit, all prewashed several times to eliminate stiffness. He began closing the jacket, watching Rose Shepherd. There was a large bulge under her black T-shirt beside her left breast. It would be the trick shoulder rig for her backup gun. She slipped into the BDU jacket.

Rufus Burroughs was rigging the black Southwind Sanctions SAS holster to his right thigh, the holster and the Desert Eagle .44 Magnum semiautomatic pistol the same rig Ruf had used that morning before the attack on Thomas Jefferson University, when Annette Burroughs had been killed, when Liz and the children had—

Holden eased both arms into his holster, then settled the harness on his shoulders. He checked the smaller of the two Barettas, the 92F Compact, bouncing the magazine, ejecting the chambered round. No bore obstructions, the action working smoothly. He reintroduced the chambered round by hand, letting the slide slam forward, safety still on, then placed the magazine up the well. The two twenty-round spares were locked securely in place in the double magazine pouch on the off-gun side, and the inverted knife sheath for the Defender hung there as well.

Holden unsnapped the twin crossover safety straps and grasped the butt of the knife, pulling it down and free. He gave the butt cap for the hollow handle a good luck twist, then resheathed the Crain knife.

Burroughs checked the Desert Eagle's action, then holstered it, checking the spare magazine in the holster's built-in pouch as well.

Rose Shepherd buckled into a black pistol belt with a Bianchi UM-84 holster and several double magazine pouches. She gave a quick check to the Detonics .45 Holden had seen on the table the night before, then holstered it, cocked and locked. There was a standard-sized Cold Steel Tanto rigged to the belt and she unsheathed, then resheathed it quickly. He had seen her earlier, before she'd gotten her boots on, with the smaller version, the mini-Tanto, strapped to her left calf.

Holden buckled on his pistol belt with the full-sized Beretta.

Rufus Burroughs pulled on a shoulder holster, his four-inch N-Frame Smith & Wesson revolver in it. Burroughs pulled the gun, checked the cylinder, reholstered it.

"Here. Ski masks are for the bad guys." Rose Shepherd handed him two black scarves. Rufus Burroughs was already tying one over his head ninja or pirate fashion. Rose—Rosie, Holden corrected himself—be-

gan to do the same. Holden folded one of them into a
triangle and did the same as well. Burroughs took the
second scarf and tied it over his face, like a bandit mask
in a cowboy movie, and, when it was secured, pulled it
down to his throat. Rosie had the second scarf in place,
then took a thin rectangular compact from the table
beside her, applying camouflage to the portions of her
face that showed above the mask.

"One of the many advantages of being black." Burroughs grinned. "If we were doin' this in daylight, I'd
still have to use it to kill the natural shine of the skin—
hell, why am I tellin' you?" And he clapped Holden on
the shoulder. Rosie passed Holden the cammie makeup
and Holden left the scarf down. He knew where to
apply the stuff, blackening his forehead, the bridge of
his nose, below his eyes and his cheekbones. He gave it
back to her.

The other four, three men and a woman, were ready
as well.

Holden took up the M16 he'd been given—U.S. property recovered from the FLNA, apparently one of the
armory-theft guns. He took up a green canvas shoulder
bag loaded with spare thirty-round magazines, then
slung it on crossbody, right shoulder to left hip.

Burroughs started from the room. Holden checked
the magazine already in the M16. Rose Shepherd
walked past him. Holden and the other four followed
her.

The van, a universal gray color, was already waiting
outside. One of the three other men got in to drive—he
was not scarved and cammie painted, but was in full
battle gear that wouldn't be visible above the level of
the windows; his M16 rested in a jury-rigged construc-

tion of wooden blocks bolted to the van floor and the side of the seat, out of view but handy.

Holden climbed in. Everyone already inside was squatting on the floor, rifle across his lap. Holden did the same. The other woman was the last inside, slamming the door after her, saying, "Ready!"

The van started moving.

It was a rough ride as they moved along the rutted dirt roads in what Holden realized would be a circuitous route from the farmhouse. Their position on the floor of the van accentuated each bump and twist. The second woman's hands were busy with something and when one of the other men lit a cigarette, in the flash of the lighter, Holden could see for an instant what she was doing. Crocheting or knitting—he could never keep the two separated in his mind although Liz had done both. Holden just shook his head. When he'd been in the SEALs he gotten rigged up for more operations and training exercises than he could remember, but never on the way to the drop point had one of his fellow commandoes been knitting.

The van kept moving. The ride smoother-seeming now, and the driver announced almost superfluously, "We're on the highway."

"They've been changing some of the stop-and-search patrols, Harry, so watch it," Burroughs cautioned.

"Gotcha, Rufe."

Holden's left forearm ached badly, but he started flexing the fingers of his left hand and massaging the area around the wound. After a while the pain eased.

He could easily tell when they reached the city; the van's interior, despite the absence of windows except at the front, was almost bathed in light by comparison.

The woman put away her knitting. One of the men drew his knife and began touching up the edge with a small set of ceramic sticks. Rose Shepherd retied her boots.

Rufus Burroughs edged over beside him. "I'm glad you're with us, David. Things shouldn't have to be this way, not here in America."

"I read an interesting letter yesterday," Holden told him, leaning back, closing his eyes against the pain in his arm. "It talked about going to hell and bailing out when you smelled the sulphur. I guess that's what this is —the sulphur."

"Brimstone. Yeah. My mother's brother was a preacher. Used to talk about hellfire and all the rest of that, used to say the world was just a place to do the best you can, for the glory afterward. I never thought much about it until Vietnam. Then I kinda hoped he was right. Guys like us, we kinda have an advantage. We've already lost everything we care about."

"Amen." Holden nodded.

And Burroughs laughed that laugh of his that Holden had come to take as part of the environment ever since his rescue from the police van. It wasn't really a laugh; Holden wasn't quite sure what exactly it was.

The van kept rolling.

"We're getting near, Rufe."

"How long, Harry?"

"About five minutes until you guys hit the bricks."

"Right. Last-minute weapons and equipment checks, people," Burroughs announced. Holden checked the security of his two Beretta pistols, that the Crain knife was properly sheathed, that the magazine for his M16 was seated.

"How long, Harry?"

"Two minutes."

"Chambers loaded, people," Burroughs announced. There was a ragged series of clicks as M16 charging handles were drawn back, then let fly forward. Holden tugged at the magazine to make certain it was secure just one more time.

"One minute, Rufe."

Holden pulled the scarf up to mask the lower portion of his face.

"Like we planned it folks," Rufus Burroughs said.

The van slowed. The woman beside the door wrenched the door open. Burroughs and Rose Shepherd were the first through and onto the street, Holden and the others right behind them, running from the van and onto the sidewalk, flattening themselves against the partially standing wall of a burned-out building, the van moving off quickly, a crunch of glass under its tires.

Holden looked to the sidewalk. He'd felt something. A rat the size of a small house-cat scurried along the curb near the gutter.

Burroughs started forward, Rose Shepherd behind him, Holden behind her, running along the edge of the wall, stopping when they reached the corner.

Rosie hissed through her bandana, "That's it if the kids had their information straight. The old Havana Hotel."

Holden snatched a quick glance around the corner over her shoulder. What had once been a six- or seven-story building was now only four stories except where the partially destroyed walls or a support post jutted defiantly upward from the light of the yellow arc lamps into the darkness beyond.

"Let's move," Burroughs commanded. Holden and Rosie Shepherd flanked him as he crossed the street. The corner lamp was shot out and a cone of semidarkness hid them, the other woman and the two other men covering.

There was a large doorway—no door left—and Burroughs plunged into it, lost in the darkness there for an instant as Rosie, then Holden, followed him inside. Holden squinted to accustom himself to the reduced light, then shouldered his M16, ready as the other three crossed, running fast, coming into the darkened doorway as well.

"Like we planned it," Burroughs said.

The woman signaled the two men and they took off with her out of the doorway and back toward the corner. They would circle the block to enter the Havana from the rear.

Burroughs was at the boundary of light and shadow in the doorway. "Move out," he hissed, breaking into a dead run close to the blown-in storefronts, Rosie after him, Holden bringing up the rear.

Burroughs stopped midway along the block, flat against the wall, his assault rifle in a raised but ready position. Rosie dropped to one knee just beside him, her rifle to her shoulder. Holden hung back, covering the opposite side of the street and their rear.

He heard Burroughs. "Movin' again." Holden started to run, dodging a little to avoid the light of an arc lamp, then ducking into a doorway as Burroughs and Rosie Shepherd stopped just ahead of him.

Holden looked up. There was the sign he had seen from the opposite side of the street, the fluorescent letters partially blown away, the sign fire-blackened.

But enough of the lettering was clear. It read HOTEL HAVANA.

His eyes caught Burroughs's eyes. Burroughs nodded, then ran up the low steps and under the arched facade, Rosie clinging to the steps against the wall, Holden jumping past her as she covered, the muzzle of her rifle snapping up for the instant he crossed its plane of fire, both Holden and Burroughs in the doorway now.

Burroughs was right about the SEALs training. It was coming back.

"Now," Burroughs rasped, stepping over the yellow warning tape that proclaimed the building unsafe for entry, then disappearing inside between the partially open doors. They were boarded where the glass had been. A fresh looking hasp had been broken off.

Holden almost tripped over the debris on the floor. The smell inside was like burnt cork.

Rosie entered, Holden still getting his eyes adjusted.

"There's a subbasement. That's where they'll be," Rosie whispered, then started ahead, Burroughs falling in after her, Holden behind him, Rosie hissing, "Trip wire—watch it."

Burroughs stopped abruptly, Holden almost bumping into him, Holden stepping over the same spot in the passageway as Burroughs did, then following on. The burnt-cork smell was stronger and there were tiny sounds, rat feet skittering along the dusty floor.

"Another trip wire," Rosie called out of the darkness, first Burroughs, then Holden stepping over it. There were a half-dozen steps, Rosie hugging to the wall side as she ascended, Burroughs and Holden behind her, then what had been another set of doors, but boards only now, the boards set in place to appear to be nailed

securely. Rosie started to edge one of the larger ones
away, Burroughs helping her, Holden covering their
rear.

There was a creaking sound; the board was about to
split. But Burroughs pushed the board back as Holden
looked. They tried another board. This one moved
freely, and Rosie slipped through the opening, Burroughs after her, Holden at the rear.

The three of them crouched just inside the inner
doorway. A vast, high-ceilinged lobby opened before
them. Where the windows were blown out, enough
light from the street got in so that objects, however
fuzzy, could be seen as darker and lighter amorphous
shapes.

Rosie jerked a thumb toward the left.

She started ahead, Burroughs beside her, Holden taking up the rear again, turning around, covering the
lobby as much as he could, then seeing nothing, running on, his rifle at high port, his left forearm consumed
with a dull ache.

They stopped before a long stairway, the three of
them flat against the wall. "There was a basement restaurant here, like I said. They called it Satan's Cellar.
The subbasement steps are on the far side of it."

She started down. Holden hoped the name wasn't
prophetic.

They kept to the side of the staircase, Burroughs and
Rosie on one side, Holden on the other. The staircase
wound downward. There was as yet no sign of the other
three Patriots. But they might have been trying the
other basement entrance Rosie had told them about.

They kept slowly moving, careful of each footfall,
watching for more trip wires. Finally they reached a

landing and there Rosie moved her left hand, signaling a stop. Holden had heard it too. A voice.

The subbasement was their goal, but it had seemed likely from the outset that guards would be posted in the basement itself, and the as yet unintelligible voice confirmed that.

Holden shifted his rifle to his left hand, his left arm hurting badly. With his right hand, he touched the butt of his knife beneath his right arm. He could see Burroughs nodding back in the half-light.

Holden safed his weapon, and handed it across the stairs to Rosie. Burroughs gave her his as well. Holden drew his knife, conscious of the sound of the snap closures opening. His right fist balled over the rope-wrapped synthetic handle surface. Burroughs drew a knife. Holden had recognized it earlier as a Gerber MkII.

Burroughs nodded toward the base of the stairs, indicating that Holden should go first.

Holden nodded back, then started across the landing, staying in a deep crouch, peering downward. There were two figures; he couldn't make out any details except that they had assault rifles near them. They were sitting on folding chairs near the base of the stairs. On the floor beside one of the chairs was some sort of electronic apparatus—to monitor radio signals, Holden supposed, that would be sent if the trip wires were activated.

From where they sat, they would have perfect command of the stairs and the rear of the basement. But there was a cone of light at the center of the upended crate between them, and seeing hand movement in the

light, Holden realized they were playing cards. They
weren't watching.

He heard a curse and a laugh.

Holden looked back to Burroughs, signaled that there
were two that he could see. Burroughs nodded.

Holden started down the stairs, slowly, keeping to the
railing side, the Defender knife in a rapier position in
his right fist.

He kept moving.

One of the two card players shifted position. Holden
froze. There was more laughter, the clink of a bottle.

Holden started moving again, catching a glimpse of
Rufus Burroughs at the edge of his peripheral vision,
moving down the stairs on the wall side.

Holden stopped, three treads from the bottom,
twenty feet from the two men.

He focused his mind on what lay in the subbasement,
trying to push any thought of the two men out. He
moved quickly, down the three stairs in a single stride,
one of the two men starting to turn, starting to rise,
Holden running the twenty feet separating them, lung-
ing with the knife, driving it into the man's throat just
beneath the jaw, tearing it free. The second man started
up. Holden threw himself toward him. There was a gun
in the second man's hand. Holden backslashed the knife
across his throat as their bodies slammed together, his
left arm screaming at him as he raised it, his gloved
hand going up to cover the mouth and mute the death
scream.

Holden looked behind him. Burroughs was ramming
his knife into the chest of the first man, bringing the
body down easily. Holden's man was still alive. Holden's
palms sweated and his mouth was dry. It had been a

long time since he had killed a man with a knife. He closed his eyes for a split second, then opened them as he rammed the knife up under the sternum and into the chest. The body twitched once and was still.

Holden got up, shakily, to his feet. He bent over and wiped the blade clean of blood on the dead man's trouser leg, then sheathed the Defender, snapping the safety straps closed.

Rose Shepherd was already moving through the basement, handing off the other two rifles to Rufus Burroughs, moving her own to a hard assault position, as she began checking the corners, behind the old packing crates and bales.

Holden took back his rifle, then moved toward the doorway Rose had told them about. The door was open. The stairwell beyond was pitch black, pale yellow light glowing from below but no voices audible.

Rose was beside them then.

Burroughs whispered, "We can't wait for the others. Move out."

Burroughs started down the stairs, Holden after him, Rose at the rear.

The going was slow; they were trying to move soundlessly, and the stairwell was so terribly dark that seeing the stairs themselves was impossible.

Holden almost lost his balance once, but caught himself against the wall, plaster crumbling under his weight. He stood stock still. There was no sound from below. If people were down there listening, they'd probably attributed the noise to rats.

Holden, Burroughs, and Rose Shepherd started moving again, the light better as they neared the base of the stairs. Voices were finally audible, but sounded strangely far away, unintelligible.

Rose was beside him, her whispered voice so low he could barely hear her. "The subbasement isn't that big. I just told Rufe. What they might have done was knock out the wall and get into the underground. There was a section of subway tunnel they started digging here just before World War II, but they abandoned the project when the Japanese bombed Pearl Harbor. They never went back to it. But there were eight or ten miles of tunnels and this section of Kirkpatrick always flooded because it was so much lower than the surrounding area, so a subbasement in this building might be at the level of an ordinary basement on the other side of the block."

Holden hissed back, "Wonderful," then started moving again.

He'd known guys who'd been tunnel rats in Vietnam. He'd never envied them moving through unending darkness waiting for someone to kill them.

They came nearly to the base of the stairs and waited. The voices were slightly louder now, but still nothing of the words could be understood. The light here was a little stronger, but not appreciably brighter.

Holden stepped down to the last stair, peered around from the stairwell.

The source of the light was about twenty-five yards off. He realized that was the reason it seemed so diffused here.

He signaled Burroughs to take a look. Rose had been right.

Holden wheeled toward the top of the stairwell. Movement.

Rose touched his shoulder.

Burroughs flattened against the opposite wall.

They waited, another telltale sound, but it could have been a rat, or a stray cat come to hunt one.

Holden saw movement and swung up the muzzle of the M16.

"Burroughs?" The knitter's voice hissed.

"Here!" Burroughs whispered back.

After a few seconds the six of them were together at the base of the stairwell. No guards were visible beyond, just the diffused yellow light in the distance. Rose insisted that the light came from inside the abandoned tunnel or from a basement in another abandoned building on the other side of the tunnel section.

Burroughs announced a decision. "Three of us go on each side of the subbasement and we link up by the hole in the wall or whatever the hell it is. If I give this signal" —and he raised his bunched right fist—"Then we go in shooting as fast as we can. All agreed?"

"Agreed." Holden nodded. Rosie, the knitter, and the other two men grunted agreement as well.

"You three stick together. Take the right. We'll take the left. Let's move out."

They started away from the stairwell.

Holden immediately behind Rosie, Burroughs in the lead, they picked their way lest they make some inadvertent noise by stepping in the debris of decades of neglect strewn about here.

Each of them had a mini flashlight, but the only light they dared travel by was the light ahead. Holden's eyes were so accustomed to the gray wash around him that he worried he'd be momentarily blinded once he reached brighter light. He kept moving.

They reached the far wall. Burroughs clung to the corner; Rosie edged ahead. Holden covered their rear again. He glanced toward Burroughs then. Burroughs moved quickly along the wall, overtaking Rosie, passing her.

At the center of the wall was a rough-cut opening, the light brighter here.

David Holden quickened his pace, joining them by the hole in the wall. Bricks were strewn about on the floor, the footing treacherous. The knitter and the two men with her reached the hole in the wall.

Burroughs signaled them to wait, then approached the hole, peered through, and passed from sight.

Holden's right fist tightened on the pistol grip of the M16, his left forearm aching badly now. His mouth was dry. He tried to read the face of his watch. It was impossible. He promised himself that if he got out of this alive, he'd get one of the Patriots who wouldn't be instantly recognized to take some of the money from the safety deposit box and find a jewelry store that stocked Rolex watches. If he was now in the commando game again, he needed one.

Burroughs, slipping back through the hole in the wall, hissed to Rosie and Holden, "About fifteen of them just beyond the tunnel in a basement on the other side. You were right about that tunnel network, Rosie. There's one guard I saw about a hundred yards down in the tunnel. We're gonna have to hit quick, because I've got a feelin' they're all over down here. Then we're gonna have to run like hell. I saw lights at intervals all along the tunnel in both directions. But we picked the right spot. There's some kind of meetin' going on just across from us. Documents and shit all over a table and a lot of talkin'. There's somethin' goin' down. I heard someone mention 'Plant Wright.' "

"The nuclear generating plant," Rosie whispered. "Shit."

"Yeah—and deep," Burroughs added. "We go in, grab everything in sight, take a prisoner if we can, and make a run for it back the way we came."

"How are you gonna know who to take prisoner?" Holden interrupted.

"Just shootin' craps, David."

"All right," Holden agreed.

"Ready?" Burroughs asked, but he didn't wait for an answer. He raised his fist, the prearranged signal, then dived through the wall opening, Holden shoving Rosie Shepherd aside and going right after him.

Burroughs was in the tunnel, Holden entering it; the guard Burroughs had seen was visible a hundred yards or so down. Holden snapped to Rosie, "Get him!"

The gunfire started then as if everyone had agreed in advance—on both sides—to start shooting at some specified time. Burroughs's M16 spit fire, Holden beside him, both men spraying their assault rifles into the fifteen men in the yellow light inside the basement on the opposite side of the tunnel, some of the lights—bare overhead bulbs—shot out, the men around the table returning fire, M16s, submachine guns, and handguns licking tongues of fire into the gathering darkness, Rosie shouting, "Got the guard!"

The knitter and her two men pushed through under their fire, onto the concrete basement floor, fanned out, and fired in all directions as the FLNAers not killed in the first volleys took cover. Holden dropped his spent magazine to the floor, changing sticks, dodging right

and ducking behind some packing crates. Burroughs
moved left, Rosie stayed beside the opening. "Men
coming up the tunnel! Both sides of us! Hurry!" Her
M16 opened up.

Holden shouted to her, "Take this! Catch it!"

Rosie wheeled toward him as he safed his M16 and
tossed it toward her. She caught it with her left hand.
Holden turned away, hearing both assault rifles open up
in her hands as he snatched the full-sized 92F from the
holster at his right side, twisting his left arm upward—
his forearm screamed at him with pain—and his left fist
closed over the butt of the smaller Beretta. He popped
the safety strap, the thumb break, then ripped it from
the leather through the trigger guard break.

A 9mm in each hand, Holden started forward, while a
heavy assault rifle poured its fire into the packing crates
behind which he moved. Holden spotted a target and
fired, a dark-featured man in profile who himself was
firing toward the opening into the tunnel. A double tap
from the pistol in Holden's right fist spun him around,
his M16 on full auto and firing into the ceiling, blowing
another of the lights, chunks of brick or concrete and a
spray of dust falling all around them. Holden stabbed
both pistols toward the man, firing again and again, the
body slapping back into the table, which collapsed under his weight.

Holden ran, gunfire tearing into the table, Holden
snapping off shots toward the source, not looking to see
if he hit, the smaller Beretta going to his waistband, his
left hand closing over the dead man's M16, the fist
locked on it. Holden ducked, pointed the muzzle of the
92F at the dead man's right wrist and fired twice, avert-
ing his eyes from the spray of blood and possibly bone,

feeling the left side of his neck suddenly go moist. Holden grabbed the rifle, rolling away across the floor, his left forearm hitting the floor surface at the wrong angle. Involuntarily he screamed.

He tucked back behind a stack of packing crates as he fired out the 92F, blindly working the slide release, stabbing the pistol into the Bianchi holster at his hip. He found the M16's magazine release, buttoned out the spent or partially spent magazine—he hadn't counted his enemy's shots—and started ramming a fresh one home.

A man charged toward him, a submachine gun blazing tongues of fire into the gray darkness, almost blindingly bright, the packing crates ripping and tearing under the impacts. There was a loud boom, then another. Holden glanced left as he worked the charging handle of the M16. It was Burroughs, his big Desert Eagle .44 flashing flamethrower-length tongues of fire each time it discharged. Burroughs dropped another of the FLNAers with a single shot. "One helluva gun," Holden said under his breath.

He edged forward, seeing a target pop up from behind packing crates about fifteen feet away and start to fire. Holden fired, blowing three short bursts into the head and shoulders, the body toppling back.

There was no gunfire from inside the basement.

There was gunfire from the entrance through the wall. Rosie Shepherd shouted, "We've got big trouble. About two dozen guys on each side of us, advancing as fast as they can!"

Holden looked toward her. The knitter and one of the other two male Patriots had joined her.

Burroughs told the other man, "Go help 'em out,"

then called to Holden. "So much for taking prisoners, huh?"

Holden was already reloading the big Beretta as he bent over one of the FLNAers. "This guy's from the Middle East or I'm from Mars."

"Not the first one we've found. That guy who calls himself 'the Vindicator', the guy that was on TV?"

"Yeah?"

"Might be Russian."

"Wonderful," Holden observed, swapping sticks in the M16, putting the spent magazine in his belt. "Ton of paperwork here. Maps." Holden stooped over the greatest concentration of the scattered materials that had been on the demolished table as he replaced the partially loaded smaller Beretta in the shoulder rig. He kept flexing his left wrist, opening and closing the fist. His arm was killing him.

Burroughs's minilight shone across the papers. Holden squinted against it, then got out his own and flashed it up toward Rufus Burroughs. "Hmm! How do you like it?" And he laughed and so did Burroughs. "This is an engineering diagram of a nuclear reactor," Holden told Burroughs. "I had to use one of these as the basis for an illustration once."

"Check this out," Burroughs told him, passing over a notebook. The writing, in English, was almost impossibly bad, but there was a date and time, underlined and circled.

"That's about an hour from now," Burroughs said, his voice low.

"We've gotta call the FBI."

"We do and it'll all go to hell."

"What if there aren't enough of us to take care of this,

what if we screw up, huh? I'll tell you what, Rufe.
They're not going to Plant Wright on a field trip.
They're going there to blow it up. We both know that."

"Compromise, then. We go in, then alert the FBI.
Might get our collective tits in the wringer that way, but
we got it covered both ways. One of those crates I almost hid behind," he said, standing, putting a fresh
magazine into the Desert Eagle. "Check it out with
me."

"Hurry up, guys!" Rose shouted, as the gunfire started
again.

Holden followed Burroughs. With the aid of the flashlight he could see the labels on some of the crates, M16s,
ammunition, spare parts, marked U.S. PROPERTY. But
the crate beside which they stopped was the most interesting because it was half empty. Holden took out one
of the green bags, and shone his light on it. The print
was faded. There was the chemical/biological warfare
symbol, the stenciled letters US and beneath it, MASK,
PROTECTIVE FIELD M17.

"They have chlorine gas. We know that," Burroughs
murmured.

"They're using these, then," Holden said.

"Grab some."

"Check for filters," Holden advised. In the pouch on
the side of the masks—which were in mint condition—
were replacement filter elements. "We're set."

Burroughs grabbed up half a dozen of the cases, sling-
ing them over his left shoulder. Holden took a half-
dozen more and did the same.

"Let's grab the stuff off the floor," Burroughs ordered,
both of them gathering up armloads of the paperwork

and maps and notebooks. There was no time to check the bodies for anything that might prove revealing.

"Use some of the gas-mask bags," Holden suggested.

They returned to the crate, tore gas masks free of the bags, and began stuffing the bags with the captured documents. When they had all they could packed away, Burroughs said, "Let's boogie."

They started for the hole in the basement wall. The gunfire was growing stronger again when Holden tucked back beside Rose Shepherd. "What was keeping you guys?" she snapped.

"You were doing such a great job here, we didn't want to interrupt," Holden told her. He peered out. Enemy forces were gathering on both ends of the tunnel, less than fifty yards down, massing, it seemed, for an assault.

"We cover," Burroughs ordered, "while you three cross. Then you guys cover Rosie and David and me. Right? Everybody set?"

The knitter and the two men with her acknowledged. Holden took back his own M16 when Rosie offered it, one in each fist now, his left arm beyond pain but the hand still working. It wouldn't be once he stopped using it for a while.

"Go!"

The knitter and her two men drew back, Holden stepped into the tunnel, firing both M16s, Burroughs and Rosie behind him, firing in the other direction, the knitter and the two men with her running across the tunnel. Holden glanced back once saw the knitter catch one in the left leg, go down, the two men dragging her after them. They were safe across.

The knitter, her voice pain-etched, called across, "We've got you covered!"

"I'll tell ya when," Burroughs called back.

Holden had reloaded, saving the empty magazines. Rosie nodded.

"Now!"

Holden jumped into the tunnel, firing, the two men from the other team already firing. Rosie ran across, firing her M16 one-handed. Burroughs snapped off neat three-round bursts. Holden hosed out both rifles and jumped through to the other side, falling on his left arm again. They were through.

"How you doing?" Rosie was asking the knitter.

"I've done better. I don't think anything's broken, though."

Burroughs leaned down and took her rifle away, handing it to Rosie, taking the knitter up into his powerful arms as if she were only a child. "I got ya, babes," he said reassuringly. "Now—let's move, people!" Burroughs started ahead, saying, "You guys take ahead of us. Rosie. David—cover our rear. Hurry!"

They crossed the subbasement quickly, Holden and Rosie covering their rear. Burroughs called back when he and the others had started up the stairs. Holden and Rosie Shepherd quickened their pace. There had been no gunfire since they crossed the tunnel and Holden realized it was just a matter of time until the FLNAers came through into the subbasement in pursuit.

Holden and Rosie reached the base of the stairs. Burroughs called back, "We get this business over, we're comin' back here in force and wipe 'em out!"

Holden started to respond, but Rosie shouted, "They're coming! Move it!"

Men shapes moved through the hole in the wall. Holden fired toward them. Rosie fired. Gunfire hammered into the floor, stairs, and walls on both sides of them as they hit the stairs and backed their way up, Holden firing out both assault rifles, letting them fall to his sides on their slings, drawing the big Beretta from the hip holster. "Up the stairs, Rosie! I'll cover you! Move it!"

They exchanged a quick glance, then she ran for it. Holden fired out the Beretta in double taps, blowing the fifteenth round. When the slide locked open, Holden started up, taking the stairs two and three at a time, changing magazines in the pistol, reaching the top of the stairs. Rosie waited just inside the doorway. "Got you covered," she told him. He ducked through, loading fresh magazines into each of the M16s.

"At the stairs," she said calmly.

Holden nodded. "Now."

They stepped partly into the doorway and sprayed out their weapons, Holden smelling his rifles. Pretty soon, they'd be cooking off by themselves.

"Empty!"

"Me too!" Holden shouted. "Run for it!" He let Rosie Shepherd get ahead of him. She was changing sticks in her M16 as she ran, and Holden did the same, right behind her.

They reached the second set of stairs, no gunfire from ahead of them, taking cover there as best they could by the stairwell base. "How to burn out a barrel in ten easy lessons," Holden joked.

"You want fried eggs in the field? Try this handy dandy convenient cooking device," she laughed back.

He liked her. He wouldn't let himself do more; he promised himself that.

"Now?"

He could see them coming, working their way along the walls on both sides, on knees and elbows. In a moment someone would think of fire support from the head of the stairs toward where he and Rosie were positioned.

"Now!"

They thrust their assault rifles out and fired, hosing both sides of the basement wall, screams, answering fire, chinks of wood and plaster spraying around them. "Up the stairs, Rosie!"

"Same time you go!"

"Make it now!"

Holden started running, Rosie Shepherd beside him, both his rifles nearly empty, but as they reached the head of the stairs, he turned around, firing them out, then dropping them, grabbing Rosie by the shoulders, and forcing her ahead of him.

Running back through the boarded-up doorway, ignoring the trip wires as they moved along the passageway to the front doors, then into the light. It was a brighter gray than inside, just dawn.

The van was coming around the corner. Burroughs still carried the knitter; the rest of them were in defensive positions, waiting.

The van stopped and Burroughs put the woman inside, drawing the Desert Eagle from the SAS holster. "Move it, people!"

Holden pushed Rosie ahead of him into the van, his rifles so hot he burned himself when his wrist brushed against one at a gap between his glove and his cuff.

Burroughs swung inside, shouting, "Go for it!"

The van peeled away from the curb, men rushing out of the entrance of the Havana, firing, bullets pinging off the exterior of the van. Holden shielded Rosie Shepherd with his right arm and upper body, the van taking a corner. Holden felt it in his stomach. And then the gunfire was behind them.

"Home?"

Burroughs answered instantly. "Get us to Plant Wright, down on the river. Then get our lady here home to medical help. I got a phone number for you. Call it after you drop us off. We'll get ourselves back to the farm." Burroughs looked at Holden. "We'll try the tit-in-the-wringer ploy."

David Holden felt himself smile.

"Okay, people—everybody gets a gas mask. Christmas comes early this year," Burroughs declared.

CHAPTER
27

The ride to Plant Wright was quiet. Burroughs and Rosie pored through the captured documents. Holden, his extensive medical training from the SEALs coming in handy, did what he could for the knitter. He thought about Burroughs's remark that it all would come back, and he thought about the fight in the basement, then the gunfight and their escape. It had come back.

Holden's watch showed fifteen minutes tops before the FLNA attack was to start, if they had interpreted the captured notebook correctly. They had been so busy taking the documents and the gas masks, neither Burroughs nor Holden had thought to take some of the 5.56mm balls in abundance there. Holden had four loaded magazines left for his rifle. That was all. They would divide the injured woman's ammo among them, perhaps take some of the driver's as well, but he couldn't be left defenseless in the event of a stop or some other trouble.

Ever since the first attacks over the Christmas holidays, nuclear plants had been more heavily guarded than usual. Holden had no idea exactly how the chlorine gas would be used—it was primitive but effective—but could imagine some ways. Bombs of the gas could be dropped on the facility by low-flying aircraft or, if the FLNA had someone working in the facility, the gas could be introduced into the ductwork; then the exterior guards would be the only ones to be dealt with. The nuclear regulatory apparatus included specially trained SWAT teams, he knew. In his SEAL days he had once trained with such a team. All they did was practice for the day someone invaded a nuclear plant.

Somehow, he didn't think they would have the time to respond.

"Get us up into the heights by the old power plant and we can work our way down. There's an old eroded wash we can use for cover until we're within a couple of hundred yards of the plant fence," Burroughs instructed the driver.

"I know the place."

Holden had done all he could for the woman. The knitter needed a doctor to go after the bullet, but the bleeding was all but stopped and he had given her a shot to ease the pain. She seemed balanced between sleep and wakefulness, tossing, her eyelids moving.

Holden sat back. He asked the man who had smoked on the way in to the Eighth and Kirkpatrick site, "You got an extra smoke?"

"Sure thing," and the man tossed him a package of Camels. Holden took one, nodded, and tossed the pack back. "Need fire?"

"I got fire," he said, lighting up, nodding his thanks again. He inhaled deeply and closed his eyes, his left arm aching worse than before. But he kept moving the wrist, opening and closing the fist.

Holden searched around in the bag where he carried his spare magazines, finding the K-Bar ceramic sticks, the two sticks and the wood block bound together with a couple of rubber bands. He undid the bands, assembled the sticks to the block, then drew his knife from the sheath. Holden touched up the edge, though it didn't seem to need it, drawing the flat-ground primary edge rearward and downward. Soon, he might be drawing it across a throat. . . .

There was full daylight now, but not full sunlight. Dark clouds rumbled in and the wind rose as Holden, along with Rufus Burroughs, Rose Shepherd, and the other two Patriots, made their way down the eroded wash, the centrally tapered cylindrical stacks of Plant Wright Nuclear Facility lighter gray against the darkening gray of the sky.

Approximately halfway down the wash, rain began to fall, first as a light drizzle, but within seconds heavy and cold. Holden's arm ached.

He walked beside Rose Shepherd, her black bandana over her sodden hair, rain pouring down across her face. She was a pretty girl, and unconsciously he found himself comparing her with Liz and the thought filled him with an emotion he could not describe.

They kept moving, the clay of the wash slippery beneath their combat-booted feet, the going more arduous now.

Two thirds of the way to the bottom, where the wash was rilled heavily and a bed of gravel had formed at its center, Henry Riles, one of the two Patriots, slipped,

sliding down at least fifty yards before crashing against a
rock and stopping. Holden, Burroughs, Rosie Shepherd,
and the other Patriot moved down as quickly as they
could to reach the man.

He was unconscious, but breathing, with a bloody
gash on the left side of his forehead and along his left
cheek. Holden wiped away some of the blood. It
washed away easily in the rain, the actual gash vastly
smaller and located near the man's temple, but bleeding heavily. No bones seemed broken.

"What the hell do we do now?" the other Patriot
snarled, hammering his fist against his thigh.

"He needs medical help," Holden said, stating the
obvious. "Shit."

Burroughs said nothing for a long moment. The rain
was pouring down more heavily than before, little
streams cascading through the rills in the wash. At last
Burroughs spoke. "We don't have a choice." He looked
at the other Patriot. "You wait until we're inside the
facility. You can watch for that from here, then get him
outa the wash and call Mitch Diamond."

"Mitch Diamond?" Holden repeated quizzically.

"He runs a wrecker service. He's helped us out. And,
more important, he's got a powerful enough CB base
station that he can get into our network from here and
call the farm for help," Rosie supplied.

"Rosie," Rufus Burroughs said, "he can't take care of
him alone. Someone's gonna have to contact Mitch and
somebody's gonna have to stay with Henry here. And
one person won't be able to get Henry outa the wash.
You're elected."

"Bullshit!" Rose Shepherd snapped. "The hell I will!"

"You do what I say. That's the only way to take care of

Henry. Now, each of you give us a magazine and we're takin' all of Henry's," Burroughs said evenly.

"The two of you can't—"

"Two of us have as good a chance as three of us," Holden told her quietly. She glared at him. "It's the truth, Rosie," Holden added. What he didn't say, but was implicit, he knew, was that there was very little chance at all. The FLNA would have hit the facility by now, and in force.

Rosie threw her arms around Rufus Burrows and hugged him tight. "You take care of yourself, you big lunatic!" He thought that the water around her eyes might be more than rain now. Still on her knees in the mud, she looked at Holden. "And you, too, huh?" Pulling her glove off, she extended her right hand to him. Holden did the same. Her green eyes seemed to bore into him. "You hear me, David?"

"I hear you," Holden told her softly.

Burroughs stood, slipped, recovered his balance. "We've gotta get outta this slime. Come on, David."

"I'll be waiting outside to cover you guys," Rosie Shepherd called after them.

Rufus Burroughs never looked back. Holden did. She was still on her knees in the mud there beside the injured man, the rain falling in wind-driven sheets now. "I'll be waiting!"

David Holden kept going. . . .

They reached the level ground just before the facility's main fence, traveling along the upper edge of the wash, for the last ten minutes on knees and elbows to keep themselves from being spotted. The journey, after they'd left the others behind, took another half hour.

They stopped in the low brush seventy-five yards from the fence. There were men in U.S. military battle dress utilities patrolling along the fence, M16s visible.

"Those guys are FLNA," Burroughs said flatly. "Even before I left the force, they were patrolling out here with guard dogs. No dogs. The real guards got zapped. These guys don't have any rain gear, either."

"Maybe they're just stupid, like we are?"

"No—I don't think that's it," Burroughs said thoughtfully.

"Any brilliant ideas on getting inside?"

"Inside fence is electrified. Outside fence isn't. I took this off an FLNAer," Burroughs said, reaching a green baseball grenade out from under his BDU jacket. "Think it'll knock a hole in a fence?"

"If we get it close enough, or it'll short it at least. You saying blow our way in, shoot our way past anybody that tries to stop us, and get inside the control center?"

"Pretty much. Got a better idea?" Burroughs grinned.

"No. But I sure wish I did." Holden exhaled, his eyes closed against the creeping exhaustion, the pain in his left arm, the apprehension of imminent, violent death.

Holden looked at Burroughs. Burroughs was glancing at his wristwatch, already timing the nearest guard's tour. It took three minutes at a brisk walk on the muddy gravel to reach the end of the fence where it cornered with the next segment of the perimeter, then another three minutes back.

That gave them a safe two minutes to get over the first fence and near enough to the electrified interior fence to dump the grenade where it needed to be to blow out a chunk of the chain link. Holden took the grenade and started rigging it. The only thing he had was the rubber bands from the ceramic sharpening sticks. He used the Defender to fray them—neither too much nor too little, he hoped—then bound them over the spoon, trying to gauge by sight if they were frayed enough. If they weren't frayed enough, the spoon wouldn't pop. If they were frayed too much, the outward leverage of the spoon would pop the rubber bands before he had time to get far enough away after the pin was pulled. It and the rain were giving him the shivers.

They edged as close to the end of the brush as they could without exposing themselves, waiting until the guard passed, Burroughs ticking off the seconds audibly. "Thirty nine . . . forty . . . forty-one . . . forty-two . . ." Holden checked the grenade again, shaking his head. The thing with the grenade gave him the creeps.

"Fifty-seven . . . fifty-eight . . . fifty-nine—go for it!" And Burroughs was up, running, his rifle at high port, Holden right behind him, then beside him, Burroughs starting to sling his rifle as they neared the fence, Holden already doing it, the fence at least twelve feet high. He hadn't climbed that much chain link since he'd been a kid. The grenade under his BDU jacket was something he was terribly conscious of.

They were near enough to the fence, Holden pouring on as much steam as he could, jumping, grabbing handholds in the chain link, his left arm in agony, his toes scraping against the links, pushing him up, hands grasping quickly, Burroughs breathlessly counting, "One fifty-eight . . . one   fifty-nine . . . two . . . two-oh-one . . . two-oh-two . . ."

Holden was at the top, the barbed wire there nothing

he could do anything about, his right thigh catching on it as he swung his leg over—"Shit!"—and then his left sleeve caught, and he felt his flesh rip. Tetanus-shot time, he told himself, then remembered he'd gotten one for the arm wound. He rolled over, his left trouser leg ripping, his hands grasping for the chain link, catching a handhold, then letting go as he dropped, rolled forward to his knees, both palms flat in the mud. Holden was up, glancing back to see Burroughs caught up in the wire, ripping through, rolling over and dropping.

"I'm all right!" Burroughs hissed.

An alarm, like an air raid siren, started to sound. Holden grabbed the grenade, running as fast as he could toward the fence, dropping to his knees in the mud. His muddy gloved hand slipped when he tried to pull the pin. "Shit!" Holden tried again, the pin out, the spoon starting to snap as he set the grenade against the base line of the fence, Holden's fingers fumbling it, propping the grenade, the spoon handle quivering.

Holden was up, running, his feet slipping in the mud, the shout of a guard, Holden up again. Burroughs shouted, "Dodge right, man!"

Holden dodged right—his right or Burroughs's? Burroughs opened fire, Holden running.

Somehow he felt it before he heard it and he threw himself down into the mud, chunks of needle-sized chain link flying everywhere like shrapnel, Holden rolling onto his back in the mud. There was a hole in the bottom of the fence big enough to drive a VW Beetle through. Holden was up, swinging his M16 forward, giving a quick glance to the muzzle to assure himself that it wasn't visibly packed with mud. He moved the selector to auto and started for the hole, Burroughs shouting, "It worked! Hah!"

Holden was at the fence, which was crackling with electricity. Through the hole. One of the guards ran toward them, opening fire. Holden prayed Burroughs was right, that these weren't the real guards. He fired, fired again and again, the guard's body spinning out, going down.

The central control station was clearly marked. Holden ran for it with Burroughs beside him. The door opened, men in gas masks and fatigues pouring through the door, M16s in their hands. Holden opened fire, so did Burroughs. Two of the men went down. A third about managed to retreat through the door, but his rifle flew from his hands and he grabbed at his spine, then slumped forward.

The doorway was on a small porch made of concrete; a half-dozen steps led up to it. Holden ducked beside them, changing sticks for his rifle, the magazine fully spent. "These in short supply?"

"Go ahead."

Holden tossed it, ramming a fresh stick up the well, working the bolt. Holden pulled out the gas mask that he had inspected and fitted in the van on the way over. He wiped his face as dry as he could with the bandana he was still wearing around his neck, pulled the mask over his face, exhaled a little and popped the cheeks to seal it, his eyeholes instantly fogging, then starting to clear.

Burroughs was getting into his mask.

Holden started up the stairs, flanking the door on the left, while Burroughs, flipping the railing, taking the right as he stepped over a body, climbed up the opposite side. Holden reached down and grabbed two spare thirty-round magazines off the body nearest him. Burroughs grabbed up spare magazines as well.

Holden and Burroughs looked at each other. Burroughs nodded. Holden fired a burst through the glass in the door's top panel. Burroughs grabbed the handle, Holden kicked, and the door flew open. Holden sprayed half a magazine through the doorway, Burroughs rolling in under the level of his muzzle, firing. Holden stepped through, both of them just inside the door now.

"Convenient for saboteurs," Holden remarked, looking at a map on the wall near him that showed *You are HERE* and pointed a big red arrow at the entrance. The reactor control center was clearly marked, along a straight corridor, down two levels, and left.

Holden started ahead, Burroughs beside him, assault-rifle fire ripping into the wall beside Burroughs's head. Holden fired back; a man in a gas mask tumbled out of a doorway.

Holden stepped over the body. Burroughs said, his voice Darth Vaderish through the gas mask, "Two more magazines."

"You keep 'em." Holden kept moving, running now as he saw the stairwells. He wasn't about to try an elevator.

Burroughs ran past him, crossed the stairwell mouth, and flattened himself against the opposite wall. Holden looked down. No one. Not in sight, at least. But he didn't think that would last.

Holden took the right side, Burroughs the left. Burroughs put the M16 into his left fist, the big black Desert Eagle into his right.

Halfway down the first flight, a gas-masked face appeared around the corner of the landing. Assault-rifle fire ripped into the wall near Holden's right side, Holden dodging left, firing his rifle. Burroughs popped off two rounds from the Desert Eagle.

The body fell. Holden jumped the last three stairs, checking the body quickly for spare magazines, finding two, pouching them at his side. He tore away the gas mask. "Another one from the Middle East." Holden changed sticks in his rifle.

"A lot of professionals helping out our 'people's revolutionaries,' aren't there?"

"That's the truth," Holden agreed, walking to the next flight of stairs, keeping to the right, Burroughs on the left.

They reached the first sublevel. Men in U.S. military BDUs were lying dead in the corridor—from the gas, it seemed.

"Bastards," Burroughs snarled.

Holden started into the next flight down, keeping right again.

So far so good, he thought.

David Holden and Rufus Burroughs reached the next landing down simultaneously. There was a shout from below them and Holden ducked back. Something exploded against the wall near Burroughs—a gas grenade. Burroughs recoiled from it. Holden prayed the seal on his mask was right and that it was nothing more than chlorine or CN or CS. Holden fired down into the stairwell, two three-shot bursts, then two more, looking at Burroughs. Burroughs, barely visible through the cloud of gas, nodded back. Holden started down, Burroughs firing down the stairwell too. Bursts of 5.56mm from the M16 alternated with the single shots from the Desert

Eagle, sounding like sonic booms in the confined space
of the stairwell.

Gas-masked FLNAers stepped into the base of the
stairwell, firing, driving Holden back as bullets rico-
cheted all around him. Holden reached the landing and
huddled beside Burroughs, who put a fresh magazine
up the well of the Desert Eagle and then changed sticks
in his M16. "We've gotta blast out way through, David,"
Burroughs said. Holden was still not used to Burroughs's
voice through the mask. Holden only nodded. He
changed sticks in the M16, shifted the rifle to his left
hand for a moment, drew the smaller Beretta from the
shoulder rig, then swapped hands on the guns.

Holden looked at Burroughs. Burroughs nodded.

"Now!" Burroughs rasped through his mask.

They were up, runnning down the stairs, one on each
side, both men firing their assault rifles and their pistols
simultaneously, trying to lay down enough fire to punch
through, chunks of the walls blowing away on either
side of them. Burroughs's body, visible at the far left
edge of Holden's limited peripheral vision, took a hit,
stumbled, then continued downward. Another gas grenade exploded. Holden's M16 was empty and he drew
the big Beretta from the holster at his right hip, firing it
as they closed with a half-dozen men at the base of the
stairs. Chunks of concrete ripped from the walls as one
of the FLNA men fired his assault rifle almost point
blank, and Holden dropped to his knees, skidding, firing
both handguns, emptying the little one. He was up,
hammering the butt of the empty pistol against a gas-
masked face, firing the full-sized 92F into another
man's chest.

His pistols were empty. Holden shoved them into his

belt, the slides still locked back, his right hand grabbing for the Defender as one of the FLNAers wheeled toward him, a .45 automatic discharging into the wall inches from Holden's head. Holden rammed the Crain knife forward into the man's chest. He caught a glimpse of Burroughs picking up one of the enemy and hurling him into the far wall.

Holden reached for the fallen .45, slashing another of the FLNA men across the chest and neck to fend him off. Then the .45 was in Holden's left fist. His finger touched the trigger and he dropped another of the FLNA men with a shot to the neck.

Holden wheeled around, the blood-dripping knife in his right fist, the borrowed .45 in his left.

No more combatants.

Rufus Burroughs sagged against the far wall and slipped along its length to a sitting position, a smear of blood following the course of his body. Holden upped the safety on the .45, awkwardly but efficiently, with his left thumb, then belted the cocked and locked pistol, shifting the knife to his left hand as he changed sticks in the M16 and crossed to where Burroughs was trying to get up.

"Take it easy, man!"

"Bullshit! Help me up. I'll be all right once I'm standing up, man."

Holden, as gently as he could, leaned Burroughs forward, placing his right hand against Burroughs's abdomen. It came back covered with blood. He looked at Burroughs's back; there were at least three exit wounds. "You stay here."

"Bullshit, man! I didn't come all this way—" Burroughs didn't finish, just started to stand. Holden had no choice but to help him. Burroughs swayed, stood erect. "Faster we do this, faster you can get me to a doctor, huh?" Burroughs laughed through his gas mask.

"Right." Holden nodded, not knowing what to say. "Let me try and—"

"No time, David. Anyway, some cockamamie field dressin' won't do shit for this." Burroughs started reloading his weapons. Holden wiped the knife clean of blood, sheathed it, then reloaded his pistols. He holstered the big Beretta at his side, keeping the little Beretta and the partially spent .45 in his belt.

Burroughs lurched away from the wall. "To the left, you said before?"

"Yeah." Holden answered.

They started slowly down the left leg of the corridor, which at one point took a bend. Holden peered around it. "Holy—" A burst of automatic-weapons fire ripped into the wall beside his head as Holden pulled back, chunks of concrete block shot away, clouds of dust belching out of the walls where the bullets had impacted.

"What?" Burroughs half asked, half groaned.

Holden tucked back. "About a dozen of them. They're like a roadblock, Rufe. They're just kneeling there, their rifles up to their shoulders. The reactor control room is just behind them."

Burroughs asked, "Twelve?"

"Twelve."

Burroughs shifted left and for a moment Holden thought that his friend was going to collapse and he reached out for him, but Burroughs slammed Holden back into the wall and down. Holden, staggering, tried to retrieve his balance. "Sorry, David. The only way, man!" The Desert Eagle in his left fist, the M16 in his right, Burroughs lurched into the hallway. A fusillade of automatic weapons fire erupted. Holden heard the booming of the Desert Eagle .44 again and again. Then he was on his feet, running the few paces to the bend in the corridor, throwing himself in. He saw Burroughs ten feet down the corridor, both guns blazing, FLNAers going down, two or three of them falling back. Holden had the M16 at his hip, threw himself right across the corridor, and fired so he'd miss Rufus Burroughs. Burroughs still lurched ahead. Burroughs's guns were empty and he shouted, "America!" as he seemed to hurl himself against the remaining FLNA men, using his body mass as a weapon, the rifle in his right hand thrusting against one man's chest, as if it were a spear, the big .44 Mag crashing down across another's skull. Holden, ran along the corridor, fired until he couldn't fire any more for fear of hitting Rufus. Holden closed with two of them, firing out the M16 into one, stitching him from groin to throat, then emptying the borrowed .45 into the other. He threw down the .45 and grabbed the little Beretta.

A different sort of alarm began sounding. Holden's blood chilled as he heard the disembodied female voice, the voice more menacing because of its evenness, its lack of emotion. "Main reactor elements have reached critical temperature levels. Meltdown is imminent. Please move to your assigned emergency-exit area as quickly as possible. Close all airtight doors behind you. Extinguish all smoking materials. Turn off or disconnect any equipment capable of creating possible electrical hazards. Evacuate. Evacuate." And the message began to repeat.

Rufus Burroughs was shouting. "The control room! Get in there and stop 'em, David!"

Holden dumped the empty magazine from his rifle and rammed a fresh one up the well. The doors—like institutional kitchen doors—just beyond where Rufus Burroughs lay among a tangle of bodies, his hands working to reload his weapons, were marked, "RESTRICTED AREA—REACTOR CONTROL CENTER—AUTHORIZED PERSONNEL ONLY BEYOND THIS POINT!"

Holden stepped toward the doors.

He kicked them inward and stepped through.

Four men huddled over a bewildering array of complex lighted panels on the far end of the football-field-sized room, a plexiglass wall separating them from the doorway area. In the center of the wall were two doors.

Holden walked to the doors.

He threw the weight of his left shoulder against the left one and went through.

The door slammed. The recorded warning voice kept droning on, Holden almost oblivious to it now, the voice just a small part of an overwhelming malevolent ambience.

The four figures turned from the panels, revealing a fifth figure, a man hunched over at the shoulders, his white coveralls bloodstained. Like the other four, he wore one of the black gas masks.

"Stay right where you are!" One of the four men in mixed BDUs called out menacingly.

He held a pistol. One of the others with him held a submachine gun, the other two assault rifles. The man in white coveralls was weaponless; Holden suspected him to be one of the control-room employees, forced to aid in the sabotage.

"Get out while you can," the man who had spoken before said, his voice even, almost patient sounding. Holden recognized the voice.

"I caught you on television awhile back, didn't I?" It was the man who called himself "the Vindicator." "You're one of the FLNA bigshots, right?"

"We will have meltdown beginning in"—he paused, perhaps for dramatic effect, perhaps really to consult his watch—"in two minutes and fifteen seconds."

"That's plenty of time to die," Holden called back, his right fist bunching on the pistol grip of his M16, his left fist on the smaller of the two Berettas. "You don't know me, but your people killed my wife, my two daughters, my son. And there's a man outside who's going to die. A good man. You murdered his wife too."

"If you value human life, you'll leave now or this innocent man will be shot!" He put his pistol to the head of the man in white coveralls, shoving him to his knees.

Holden started walking, slowly.

"Leave, now!"

"So you can leave? I've got nothing to live for except this country, and for every guy like me who dies fighting you bastards, there're a hundred more ready to keep fighting. You're not leaving here alive," Holden said flatly. "You shoot your hostage, I'll shoot you." Holden kept walking, the distance to them by now almost halved.

"Kill him!"

The man with the submachine gun reacted first, as Holden had thought he would. Dodging left Holden opened up with his rifle, spraying the submachine gunner's body, causing him almost to pirouette. Holden's left leg shot out from under him. He fell, rolled, the tiled floor plowing up in chunks as one of the FLNA assault rifles commenced firing. Holden stabbed the Beretta toward his attacker, firing it empty; the FLNA man smashed back into one of the control panels. The leader grabbed the man in white coveralls and dragged him back, using him as a shield as the other man with an assault rifle threw down covering fire. Holden, hit at least once in the left thigh, had the M16 to his shoulder, firing. Holden kept himself as flat to the floor as he could, firing, firing, the assault rifleman spinning out and falling.

Holden's M16 was empty.

He pushed himself to his feet, his left leg buckling. He fell.

He stood again, using the muzzle of his empty rifle like the tip of a cane, his left hand holding to the buttstock. He rammed the empty Beretta into his trouser belt, pulling the loaded pistol from its holster, his right fist bunching tight around it. Holden started walking.

"You're a dead man!" Holden shouted.

"I'll kill him!" The leader's voice came behind a lighted wall panel almost the size of a mainframe computer.

"I'll kill you anyway." Holden reached the panel, his eyes drifting over the controls. Even if he had been an engineer, he didn't think he would have known which controls to operate to stop the impending meltdown. "You could kill thousands of people, but you like that idea, don't you?"

"I'm warning you!"

Holden reached the edge of the wall of instruments and peered around.

The leader was there, his terrified hostage held against him like a shield still.

"It's your move," Holden said, stepping out, raising the 92F and extending his arm.

The FLNA leader shot the white-suited technician in the neck. Holden fired, a spasm of pain shooting up from his leg, his first bullet ripping away the FLNA leader's right ear. The leader shoved the technician's body forward as he fell back, blood gushing from the right side of his face at the edge of the gas mask. Holden swung the muzzle on line, but the FLNA leader fired first, striking Holden in the left rib cage. Holden staggered back. The FLNA leader swayed on his feet, stabbing the pistol toward Holden. Holden steadied himself and fired, the FLNA leader taking a hit in the left side, twisting away, Holden firing again, but the center-of-mass shot spoiled as the FLNA leader's body moved, the bullet impacting the man's right arm, the pistol falling from the FLNA leader's hand. He fell back. Holden stumbled to his right knee, his wounded left leg extended.

He started to make the last shot, the FLNA leader on his knees by the wall, his whole body trembling.

Holden heard the warning message again.

He closed his eyes. He saw Liz and Meg, protecting Irene from death with their own bodies, all of them gunned down. He saw his son, Dave, fighting his mother's and sisters' killer, dying too.

Holden opened his eyes.

Using the rifle to steady himself, he got to his feet.

Holden started forward. His glance shifted to his left side. A bullet had skated across his rib cage, he guessed.

Blood, but not the kind of pain you get from a broken rib or punctured lung. He'd had both, once.

Holden stood over the technician. The man's right hand was outstretched. Holden dropped to his good knee. Written in blood on the tiled floor was part of a word. It was unintelligible. Holden touched at the body. There was no pulse.

The FLNA leader.

Holden pushed himself up. He walked toward him, stood over him. Holden said, "Tell me what to do to stop this."

"Fuck you!"

"I make about a minute. You know how much pain I can cause you in sixty seconds?" Holden holstered the 92F, then drew his knife. He reached out with his left hand, drawing the gas-masked face back.

Holden held the knife like a dagger, poised over the FLNA leader's left eye. "You have two of them, and that can be twice the pain."

Holden started to drive the knife down. "No! No!" Holden held the knife less than an inch from the portion of the mask that covered the left eye. "Wait! But you have to get me out of here!"

"What do I do?"

"You'll get me out of here?"

"Yes."

"Your word?"

"Yes."

"The panel marked 'Emergency systems.' Turn the red dial marked 'Rod Elevation' as far as it will go. That will do it. Hurry!"

"Are you sure?" Holden asked, his voice low.

"Yes!"

"You call yourself 'the Vindicator'?"

"Yes. Yes."

Holden turned the knife so the right blade-flat was in front of the FLNA leader's eyes and he could read what was written there. "Meet 'the Defender.' " Holden brought the knife down and slashed open the FLNA leader's throat, blood spraying toward Holden's eyes, but the gas mask protecting him. "Sorry, I lied." Holden let go of the man's head and mask and let the body slump away. A new recorded message had started. "Meltdown imminent! Meltdown imminent! Meltdown imminent!"

Holden picked up his rifle. He looked at the body of the technician. And now he could make out what the word was supposed to have been. *Red*.

Holden moved round the end of the wall of control panels, his eyes scanning the boards. He moved toward the one marked EMERGENCY SYSTEMS. There was a red dial labeled ROD ELEVATION. Holden began to twist it.

He twisted it as far as it would go.

The recorded message stopped.

Holden breathed.

CHAPTER
28

The rain was still falling hard. As they got through the hole in the fence, David Holden heard the sirens in the distance. There would be choppers coming in, too, he knew. "Come on, Rufe!" Holden, limping on his left leg, had Burroughs half under his left arm, dragging him, Holden's right hand locked on Rufus Burroughs's right wrist, the right arm drawn across Holden's shoulders. "Come on! We're almost there, man!"

"David. Get out."

"No," Holden hissed through his teeth.

They were to the scrub brush now. "We're home free, Rufe!"

"Put me down."

Holden stumbled in the mud. Both men fell.

"I'm not getting up, David," Burroughs whispered. Blood trickled from the left corner of his mouth. Holden wiped it away with his hand. Burroughs coughed. Blood spilled out more profusely now.

Holden knelt, Burroughs's head against his chest. "You can make it, Rufe."

"Know—know why I wanted you for this so bad, David?"

"My wonderful personality," Holden said, forcing a laugh. "Don't waste your energy talking, Rufe. Come on—I'll get you—"

"For when this happened. And it had to. Take—take over—for me, huh?" And Rufus Burroughs made that laugh of his, the blood flow increasing. "Take care of Rosie, David. And—and make those FLNA bastards—make 'em—make 'em—"

Rufus Burroughs's head lolled back, his eyes wide open and the rain falling into them, the flow of blood from his mouth slowing.

"David!"

It was Rosie Shepherd's voice.

The rain seemed to be falling harder. David Holden's eyes filled with tears and he hugged his dead friend's head to his chest, the palm of his right hand, as he held Rufus Burroughs, feeling the patch sewn there. Holden's fist bunched tight over it. It was the flag.

Scott McKenna, taking short but deep breaths, tested the hand-cuffs.

The question was—could he do it? There was only one answer: *I had better!*

Closing his eyes, McKenna began to inhale slowly, taking long and very deep breaths and concentrating on an invisible spot in the center of his forehead. He was not only invoking the Absolute, he was very rapidly increasing his Chi and using self-hypnosis to open the reserves of energy stored by the pineal gland. In the parlance of the ninja, he was Stroking the Death Bird.

The fifth and final stage of the Hsi Men Jitsu, the Way of the Mind Gate, rushed to the front of his consciousness as he tested the two links holding the handcuffs together. Once this fifth stage of *tensui* had fully established itself, McKenna was pure strength, total energy. He was one with the Tao. With supreme confidence he exerted steady pressure on the links. One of the links snapped. McKenna continued the pressure. In a few more seconds his wrists were free.

McKenna noted the positions of the six gunmen. Jody Karl and Vito Gallucci had piled the contents of the desk drawers onto the top of the desk and were absorbed in going through papers and other items. Vito Gallucci was by the side of the desk and Karl stood in front of it.

Ellis Joost had pulled several dozen books from one of the bookcases and was thumbing through them while Pete Ratta and Virgil Dudenbossle continued to pull files, booklets, charts, and advertising materials from the wooden filing cabinets.

Nick Flipps was only seven feet from McKenna. His eyes were on Karl and Gallucci, across the room.

McKenna's attack was so fantastically fast that Raymond Gordel and Victor Jorges never saw him leave the crate. Neither did Nick Flipps. The goon had time only to turn his head and see the Ninja Master's descending arm. He felt only a microsecond of pain; then he was sinking into unconsciousness and dying from the terrible sword-ridge hand that had chopped him in the left side of the neck and ruptured his jugular vein and carotid artery.

Pete Ratta and Virgil Dudenbossle caught sight of McKenna from the corner of their eyes and, still in a state of surprise, were swinging around to face him, the stick-thin Dudenbossle reaching for the 9mm Astra he had shoved into his belt.

Pete Ratta's hand was reaching for a 9mm Arminex Trifire auto-loader under his coat when McKenna reached him and the now-worried Dudenbossle, who almost succeeded in lining up his weapon with McKenna's stomach. The Ninja Master's right arm shot out and his fingers tightened around Dudenbossle's right wrist, pushing the Astra pistol to one side. Simultaneously, McKenna slammed his right knee upward—the savage uplift crushing Dudenbossle's testicles. The hood uttered a loud, choked cry as the Astra slipped from his limp fingers and fell to the floor.

The Arminex Trifire autoloader was half out from underneath Pete Ratta's coat, but it was too late. McKenna's left hand chopped against the right side of his head, the Shuto sword-ridge blow as effective as a hammer hitting his jaw.

McKenna had killed Flipps and taken out Dudenbossle and Ratta in only ten seconds—a very short time, yet long enough to alert the three other hoods.

The bucket-headed Ellis Joost had a lot of courage but little common sense. He charged McKenna (who had picked up Dudenbossle's Astra) and snapped off a shot with his 9mm large-frame Llama pistol, firing only a micromoment after the Ninja Master threw the Astra pistol.

A ninja is trained in Ugokasu Jitsu, the art of "moving" or throwing, whether the object be a brick, a stone, or a bottle. Or a semiautomatic pistol.

The butt end of the Llama autoloader struck Ellis Joost just above the bridge of the nose and instantly switched off his consciousness. His 9mm full metal jacket bullet cut through McKenna's coat and shirt on the right side, the chunk of metal coming within .79th of a millimeter of touching his flesh. The slug ripped through the back of his coat and hit the east wall.

As Joost started to sink to the floor, Jody Karl yelled, *"Kill the son of a bitch!"* and fired wildly at the Ninja Master. McKenna charged toward them with great speed, ducking and dodging from side to side with incredible agility. Karl's big magnum revolver boomed, the .357 flat-nosed bullet cutting air an inch below McKenna's left armpit and only half an inch from his upper-left rib cage.

Karl did his best to step back and trigger off another round, but he had hesitated a fraction of a second too long. Jumping several feet into the air, McKenna twisted his body and executed a perfect right-legged spinning dragon kick. The sole of his foot shot into Karl's midsection like a battering ram, the dynamite blow knocking the hood off his feet and giving him the worst stomachache of his life.

Pete Ratta might have succeeded in wasting the Ninja Master if he had been an experienced gunsel. Instead, he made a fatal mistake by wanting to be absolutely certain that his bullet would hit the target. At the same time that his finger was squeezing the trigger of his Arminex Trifire pistol, McKenna grabbed his right wrist and pushed the revolver to one side, the magnum exploding when the muzzle was pointed toward the ceiling.

Gallucci tried to free his wrist from McKenna's left hand and at the same time let the Ninja Master have a left uppercut. He failed in both attempts, although he didn't have time to dwell on his failure.

McKenna's right hand, formed into a Mao Shou, the eighth of the nine hand forms, streaked straight toward Gallucci's throat. Three fingers stabbed into the jugular notch, the "soft spot" in front of the neck just above the top of the breastbone. Within the space of an eye blink, Gallucci's tracheal cartilages were crushed and he was choking to death.

Gordel and Jorges, still sitting on the wooden crates, stared at McKenna and the quivering and dying hood with all the awe most people would reserve for a newly arrived alien stepping out of a flying saucer. Not only had McKenna freed himself from his hand-cuffs, but in minutes he had slammed all six hoods, moving so fast they had not been able to keep track of him. McKenna had a handcuff around each wrist, and it was plain that he had actually broken—*broken!*—one of the links! What kind of man had Scott McKenna become?

The Ninja Master picked up the handguns and deposited them on one of the wooden outrigger crates.

"Scott, how did you do it?" asked Gordel in a small voice. "How could you pull those links apart—some kind of ninja trick?"

McKenna moved over the the stone-dead Nick Flipps and took the key to the handcuffs from the right side coat pocket of the corpse.

"It wasn't a trick," McKenna told Gordel and Jorges, both of whom had gotten to their feet. "Let's just say it was mind over matter. Turn around so I can remove the handcuffs."

McKenna freed Gordel and Jorges.

"Keep them covered. The two I only knocked out will be able to take their wounded friends out of here—after I am finished with them." He pointed to Pete Ratta, who was still unconscious on his back, then at Ellis Joost, who was lying facedown.

The four other hoods were in far worse condition. In fact, Nicholas Flipps and Vito Gallucci could not have been worse off: they were dead. Jody Karl, kicked in the stomach, and Virgil Dudenbossle, kneed in the testicles, were in a world of agony.

Ray Gordel picked up Pete Ratta's Arminex Trifire autopistol.

"What are you going to do with them, Scott?" he asked. "God almighty, I think two of them are already dead."

"They are," replied McKenna. "I meant to kill them. We're in no danger from the authorities. The others can't tell what happened here, not without incriminating themselves.

"Who is Lombardo?" asked McKenna.

"I was going to tell you about him." Gordel sounded embarrassed. "We weren't going to accept your money without letting you know what we're up against. Charles Lombardo is a bigshot attorney in Tampa. He's also looking for the *Santa Francesca*. His father is Vincent 'The Crusher' Lombardo, the semi-returned Chicago mobster. You've heard of him. He's supposed to control 'The Outfit' in Chicago."

"One of you get some ice water." McKenna looked down dispassionately at Pete Ratta, then turned to Gordel. "You can give me the details about Lombardo later."

"Scott, somehow Lombardo knew you were going to come to Tampa," Gordel said, sounding worried. "Remember how one of them called you 'ninja boy'?"

McKenna put a finger to his lips. Quickly, he walked over to a surprised Gordel and whispered in his ear. "Watch what you say. I think this office or your apartment has been bugged."

After Jorges returned with a pitcher half filled with water and half filled with ice cubes, McKenna dragged Ellis Joost across the floor and let him sag next to Peter Ratta. It didn't take long to awaken both men with the ice water. Slightly dazed, they sat up and looked at the Ninja Master in fear.

"Where are your cars parked?" McKenna asked in a pleasant voice.

Ellis Joost, who had a red lump above the bridge of his nose, glared at McKenna. Ratta, rubbing the side of his head, said nothing.

"I asked a question; I want an answer—or would you prefer I break your fingers one by one?" He looked at Joost, who had recovered more quickly than Ratta had.

"A quarter of a mile to the northeast," Joost muttered, cautiously feeling the lump on his forehead. "We parked under some palm trees."

McKenna said to Gordel and Jorges, "Keep your guns trained on these two. If either one tries to run—kill him." He turned back to Joost and Ratta. "Pick this creep up"—he pushed at Dudenbossle with the tip of his foot—"and the one in front of the desk and sit them on the couch. Don't concern yourselves with the other two. They're dead. *Move!*"

It was easier for Joost and Ratta to get Jody Karl to the couch. By the time Karl was seated the pain in his stomach was bearable. He was fully aware of the danger he and his men were facing. What could he possibly tell Chuckie Lombardo—that Scott McKenna had pulled his handcuffs apart and then slammed out all of them, killing Nick and Vito in the process?

"We—only follow orders," Karl mumbled to McKenna, hoping to get on his good side. "We don't have anything against you guys personally."

The Ninja Master's move was extremely fast. His right hand, formed into a Seiken forefist, struck Joost in the solar plexus. The blow was light and Joost braced himself for the real attack, which did not come. All he received was a slight smile from McKenna, who had just given him a Hsin Chuan heart punch, one of the nine fatal blows of the Dim Mak Way, commonly known as the "Ninja death touch."

Ratta also assumed that McKenna was toying with them. He didn't flinch when McKenna struck him lightly in the center of the chest. The blow had been so light that he had hardly felt it. Ratta didn't know it, but he had just received a fatal Fei Chuan lung punch and had only two days to live. Nervously, he wondered what McKenna would do next.